The Other Side of
Horizon

RAVINDER PAL SINGH

INDIA · SINGAPORE · MALAYSIA

ISBN
Paperback 979-8-89632-420-1
Hardcase 979-8-89777-634-4

Contents

1. The Ambulance Driver   9

A drunken argument among friends attending their college friend's wedding takes a chilling turn when they hear the gripping and mysterious tale of an ex-ambulance driver.

2. In the Mouth of Madness   23

Three troubled friends, a brand-new car, and a fatal accident that defies reality. Was it all a dream, or did they witness something beyond explanation?

3. The Meeting   45

A young writer returns to India after eight years to cover a series of murders but deems his trip a failure. That is until the very last day when he reconnects with a girl from his past, spending an evening that changes everything.

Preface

The Other Side of Horizon

by Ravinder Pal Singh

Do you truly believe that the legends of the supernatural, the tales of mythical entities, are mere figments of the Collective Unconscious?

"You can dismiss them as nothing more than a horizon—an illusion, an imaginary line that holds no place in reality. Or… you can choose to believe that no horizon is ever too distant, too unreachable, that you cannot rise above it or venture beyond."

Dare to step beyond the boundaries of imagination.

Overview

Mention ghosts, fate telling, premonitions, and other supposed mysteries of the paranormal and supernatural, and most people will dismiss them as mere figments of imagination. Yet, there are rare moments when some of us experience events that defy scientific explanation, events that linger on the very edge of perceptibility, leaving us unsettled and questioning reality.

The Other Side of Horizon is a collection of short supernatural horror stories that take a different approach to fear. While most people associate horror with blood and gore, these stories focus on a more gripping sense of trepidation and precariousness. They delve into the kind of fear that does not require violence to terrify but instead thrives on an overwhelming sense of inexplicable dread.

The terror in these stories is subtle yet deeply unnerving, crafted to unsettle your mind rather than shock your senses. They explore the fragile boundary between reality and the unknown, where fear becomes a lingering presence, haunting your thoughts and challenging your perceptions.

This is a collection for those who seek the intangible, the eerie, and the unexplainable, a journey into a world where the most terrifying experiences are the ones you cannot fully understand.

About the Author

Ravinder Pal Singh resides in the serene landscapes of Jammu and Kashmir with his parents. He holds a B.Tech in Information Technology from Chandigarh Engineering College. After earning his degree, Ravinder explored various professional avenues, working with several companies before embarking on his entrepreneurial journey. Currently, he serves as the Tech Head (Research & Development) at Tek Chand & Sons.

Storytelling has been a cherished part of Ravinder's life since his childhood. He fondly recalls weaving tales for his little cousins, who listened with wide-eyed wonder as his words transported them to fantastical worlds. Their joy and awe ignited a lasting love for narrating stories.

Ravinder's passion lies in horror, mythology, and drama, with horror holding a special place in his heart. His fascination with the supernatural began in childhood, listening to eerie tales that both startled and intrigued him. The blend of fear, mystery, and the unknown captivated him deeply, shaping his imagination and creative instincts.

When asked why he gravitates so strongly toward horror, Ravinder admits it's the thrill of venturing into the uncharted, the strange, the fearful, and the otherworldly that leaves him spellbound. This lifelong fascination inspired him to translate his love for the supernatural into writing, culminating in this debut collection of short horror stories.

Ravinder eagerly looks forward to sharing more of his work, continuing to explore the depths of fear and wonder that have captivated him since childhood.

****Special thanks to Deepanshi, Romael, Rajan, Harsh, Asees, Sukham, and Blue for believing in my writing.**

The Ambulance Driver

Two months had passed since my graduation day, and life had begun to settle into a routine. I found myself attending the wedding of a close friend, Jaideep Singh Bajwa, in the village of Doraha, Punjab. This was not an ordinary wedding, but a grand celebration reflecting the wealth and status of Jaideep's family. His father, a prominent landlord in the region, had ensured that every detail of the event was perfect. The night sky stretched endlessly above us, with stars scattered across it like glittering jewels. The moon cast its soft glow over the expansive garden, illuminating everything with a serene light.

The garden where the celebrations were unfolding was vast, filled with ornate decorations that exuded elegance. Bright fairy lights adorned the trees, while silk drapes swayed gently in the cool breeze. Everywhere, the rich scent of marigold and jasmine flowers mingled with the crisp aroma of eucalyptus, creating a heady mixture that made the air feel alive.

Guests were scattered across the venue, laughing and chatting, their voices blending with the rhythmic beats of Punjabi music. On the dance floor, people swayed and spun to the lively tunes, their faces glowing with happiness. It was a night that celebrated not only the union of two people but also the spirit of community and friendship.

At the far end of the garden, away from the crowd, a large round table was reserved for our group. Jaideep had set it up for his closest college friends, ensuring we had a space to indulge in carefree conversations and reminisce about old times. Waiters hovered nearby, bringing trays of snacks and drinks as instructed by Jaideep. Alcohol flowed freely, and the others at the table indulged eagerly. I, however, refrained, as I always did. Alcohol had never been part of my life due to my allergy to it, but I never missed out on the fun. Being with my friends and engaging in their lively banter was more than enough for me.

Jaideep made frequent visits to our table, sitting with us briefly before attending to other guests. By the time the clock struck ten, the celebration was in full swing. The music had grown louder, and the dance floor was crowded with guests, their laughter echoing through the night. The energy of the evening was infectious, and it felt as if the entire world was caught in the joyful rhythm of the wedding.

Jaideep returned to our table once more, but this time he was not alone. A tall, imposing man followed closely behind him, stepping into the glow of the lanterns that illuminated our group. I had noticed him earlier in the evening. His presence was hard to ignore, not just because of his size but also because of the quiet authority he exuded. He stood well over six feet tall, with a body that seemed carved from stone. His face was framed by a long beard and mustache, giving him the appearance of a warrior from another time. His turban was neatly tied, and his traditional attire-kurta-pajama fit him perfectly, lending him a regal air.

"This is Billa, also known as Zaildar," Jaideep said with a grin. "He is family and takes care of everything in our family."

Billa greeted us with a deep "Sat Sri Akal," his voice calm and resonant, commanding respect without effort. There was a quiet strength in him, the kind of strength that does not need to be announced. Jaideep spoke of him with pride, claiming that Billa was the strongest man he knew. None of us doubted the truth of his words. Billa's very presence was enough to convince anyone that he was capable of extraordinary feats.

He took a seat across from me, his large hands resting lightly on the table. When a waiter approached with a tray of drinks, Billa reached for a glass of juice, ignoring the array of premium alcohol. His choice of beverage mirrored my own preference, and for a moment, I felt a sense of kinship with him.

The initial pause that followed Billa's arrival soon faded, and we returned to our lively conversations. Our discussions meandered from topic to topic, touching on everything from politics to college memories. Eventually, the conversation took a familiar turn towards the supernatural. Ghost stories and tales of paranormal experiences were shared with enthusiasm.

The table quickly divided into two groups. Some of us believed in the existence of ghosts and spirits, while others dismissed such things as mere superstition. The believers spoke of haunted houses and eerie encounters, trying to convince the skeptics. The skeptics, in turn, offered logical explanations for every story, insisting that the supernatural was nothing more than a product of the imagination.

As always, I found myself acting as the mediator, trying to maintain a balance between the two sides. It soon became clear that the believers were losing ground. None of them had firsthand experiences to back up their claims, and the skeptics were quick to dismantle every story with reason and logic.

Just when it seemed the discussion was reaching a predictable end, Billa, who had been silently listening until now, cleared his throat. His deep voice broke through the chatter, drawing everyone's attention.

"I have a story," he said, his voice steady but carrying the weight of something unspoken. "And this one is not just a story. It is something that happened to me."

The lively conversation came to an abrupt halt. The music and laughter from the dance floor seemed distant now, as if the night itself was holding its breath. All eyes turned towards Billa, waiting in silence for him to continue. There was a tension in the air, a strange mixture of curiosity and unease. I could see all eyes fixed on Billa, It was perhaps the curiosity about what kind of incident this calm big man was about to state. Suddenly the music became louder and I could hear the shouts coming from the dance floor but Billa gave this no attention, and began to speak in the same calm, droning monotone in which he had started the conversation.

"It happened ten years ago," Billa began, his voice low and measured. "Back then, I was not working for Jaideep's father. I was driving an ambulance for a hospital, working on a contract basis. My job was to transport dead bodies from one place to another."

He paused, letting the gravity of his words sink in.

"It was not an easy job, but when you have a family to support, you do what you must."

The flickering lantern light cast shifting shadows across his face, making his features appear sharper, almost haunted.

"That night, around eleven, I received a call to move a body from Doraha to Kharar. It was a routine job, nothing out of the ordinary. And, as always, I was alone."

He allowed the silence to linger on the word "alone," as if it held a deeper significance. The weight of his story settled over us, and none of us dared to interrupt. The garden, once filled with laughter and music, now felt strangely still as we waited for Billa to continue.

Billa's voice flowed steadily, pulling us deeper into his tale. The wedding celebrations around us felt distant, as though they belonged to another world. His expression remained composed, yet there was a heaviness in his eyes, like someone sifting through memories that never quite left.

"That night started like any other," he began, leaning slightly forward. "The road from Doraha to Kharar was a far cry from what it has become now. Back then, it was rough and narrow, with long patches of potholes that could jar even the sturdiest vehicle. There were no restaurants, no lights, no signs of life along the way, only trees lining both sides of the road. During the day, you might see a few travelers passing through, but at night, it became a deserted stretch where not even a dog wandered."

He paused, letting us picture that lonely path in the stillness of night.

"Despite how difficult the road was, there was something peaceful about it. The cool breeze that night brought a sense of relief after a long, tiring day. Dark clouds gathered above, and occasional flashes of lightning flickered in the distance, illuminating the sky for a fleeting

     THE OTHER SIDE OF HORIZON

moment. It was the kind of night that made you want to drive slow and let the silence settle over you."

His large hands rested firmly on the table as he continued. "I drove carefully, keeping my speed low to avoid the bumps that littered the road. With every jolt of the ambulance, I reminded myself that there was a body in the back. One careless mistake, one bad bump, and it could slide off the stretcher. That was something I could not afford."

The weight of his words lingered over us, making the chill of the night air more pronounced.

"For a while, the drive was quiet. The road ahead was empty, and the trees swayed gently in the breeze. My mind drifted to the sky, where the clouds shifted, exposing patches of starlight between them. For a moment, I allowed myself to admire the beauty of the dark clouds against the distant flashes of lightning."

Billa stopped and rubbed his hands together, as if trying to shake off the memory of that night. "It was then that I noticed something. A dark shape stood at the side of the road, just a little ahead of where I was driving."

We all leaned closer to him, fully absorbed now, each of us imagining the scene through his eyes.

"As I got closer, the shape became clearer. It was a woman. She appeared to be in her late thirties, standing completely still. She was wearing a shimmering white outfit that reflected the faint light from the sky. She lifted her hand slowly and waved, as if asking for a ride."

He stopped briefly, his gaze lingering on the center of the table, lost in thought. "It was not unusual to see someone waiting by the road at that hour, hoping to catch a ride. Public transportation was scarce in those parts, and not many could afford their own vehicles."

Billa exhaled deeply. "I was young back then, and I was about to stop for her without a second thought. But something inside me hesitated. Something felt... wrong. A woman alone on a deserted road that late at night did not seem normal. My mind filled with possibilities. What if this was a trap? What if there were others waiting in the dark, ready to ambush me as soon as I stopped?"

His voice grew quieter, but it carried the weight of that moment. "I wrestled with myself. What if she was just someone in need, stranded and desperate? But the thought of falling into a trap outweighed my instinct to help."

He looked at us with a grim expression. "I made my decision. I kept driving. I did not stop or even look back."

The silence around the table was heavy, as if each of us was trying to imagine what we would have done in his place.

"The decision left me unsettled," Billa continued, his voice thoughtful. "As I drove on, doubt began creeping in. I could not shake the feeling that I should have helped her. What if she was in real trouble? My mind was so consumed

     THE OTHER SIDE OF HORIZON

with these thoughts that I stopped paying attention to the road."

His eyes flickered with the memory of that moment. "The ambulance bounced over a rough patch, jostling the stretcher in the back. That is when I heard it."

He looked at us one by one, making sure we were following every word. "It was a faint sound, like a soft thud, coming from the back of the ambulance. I thought the body had fallen off the stretcher because of my careless driving."

Billa shifted slightly in his chair. "I kept one hand on the steering wheel and reached for the small window between the front cabin and the back compartment. When I looked through, I was relieved to see the body still in place. It had not moved an inch."

He paused for a moment, rubbing the back of his neck. "But the relief did not last long. I told myself to focus on the road and drive more carefully, but my thoughts kept drifting back to that woman. I kept wondering if I had made the right choice by not stopping. The unease stayed with me, gnawing at the edges of my mind. I didn't want to think about it and so I started paying more attention to the bad road and drove with more focus. I tried to concentrate hard but it was not long before the woman was once again in my mind and I found myself arguing with myself on the decision I had made back then. I was not sure if my decision to not stop and help her was the right one."

His voice lowered. "And then it happened again. I heard the same sound from the back of the ambulance. This time, it was louder, and it came in three distinct intervals like the first time."

Annoyed by myself, I said to myself "I should have learned from my mistakes and paid more attention on the road".

This time I was sure that the body had fallen as I heard it loud and clear. In a hurry I opened the back window once again to find the body intact in its place on the stretcher, not having moved an inch.

A chill ran down my spine as Billa spoke, and I could see that the others felt it too.

"I told myself it was nothing, just my mind playing tricks on me. But deep down, I knew it was not. Something was off. I reached for the small window again, expecting to find the body out of place this time."

He took a deep breath, his large hands gripping the edge of the table. "But when I looked, the body was exactly where it had been before. It had not moved at all."

Billa paused, and his eyes scanned our faces, as if to make sure we understood what he was saying. "I sat there, confused and on edge. I knew what I had heard. I was not imagining it. But there was no explanation."

He leaned back slightly, as if reliving the tension of that night. "Just as I tried to convince myself it was nothing, I heard it again. My eyes moved instinctively to the rear

     THE OTHER SIDE OF HORIZON

side mirror of the ambulance because it was coming from outside, the right side of the ambulance. Billa took a long breath and his eyes darted from left to right. There was a strange uproar in his calm face and his earlier droning monotone was a little shaky with a touch of emotions in it. All the twelve eyes were fixed at Billa with their ears focused so as not to miss a single word. Billa took a small pause and started once again.

This time, I was ready. I listened carefully, and I knew where the sound was coming from."

His gaze darkened as he said, "It was not from inside the ambulance; it was coming from outside, right beside the vehicle."

The silence at our table was complete. Nobody moved, nobody spoke. We were all waiting, our hearts racing, to hear what came next.

Billa sat still for a moment, his face expressionless, as if searching for the right words. The weight of the memory seemed to press down on him, and we waited in silence, knowing instinctively that what came next would not be easy to hear.

"I glanced at the side mirror," he said, his voice low and deliberate, "and what I saw was impossible to believe. No matter how many times I have thought about it since that night, I still cannot find a reasonable explanation."

His eyes darkened as if the memory was still as vivid as the moment it happened. "I was driving at a cautious speed of forty kilometres an hour. Even though I had been careful, I felt a chill run through me the second I saw what was reflected in that mirror."

Billa exhaled slowly, as if the act of telling the story was draining him. "There she was. The same woman I had seen by the roadside. But she was not walking. She was running beside the ambulance on all fours, moving with a speed that no human should possess."

We sat frozen in our seats, hanging on to his every word, the image forming in our minds more clearly than we wanted it to.

"I stared in disbelief, convinced that my eyes were playing tricks on me. But it was no illusion; I could hear her nails, or whatever those things were, scraping against the metal of the ambulance and tapping at intervals, as if she was trying to get me to stop, the sound sharp and deliberate, like someone knocking on a door. Billa's expression remained calm, but his hands tensed slightly as he relived the moment. "Then she spoke," he said, his voice quieter now. "She called my name."

A collective chill ran through us. There was something deeply unsettling about the idea that the strange woman knew his name.

"Her voice was unlike anything I have ever heard before," Billa continued, his eyes distant. "It was hoarse and broken, as if it belonged to someone who had not spoken in years. It was hollow and unnatural, like the

     THE OTHER SIDE OF HORIZON

sound of wind howling through a crack in a door. It did not belong to this world."

He paused for a moment, as if those words still echoed in his mind. "I wanted to believe it was all some kind of hallucination, a trick of the mind. But I knew it was not. The way she moved, the way her voice sounded, everything about her was real and impossible at the same time."

Billa leaned forward slightly, his gaze locked on ours. "In that moment, instinct took over. I pressed the accelerator as hard as I could, and the ambulance roared to life. I did not care about the bumps or the potholes anymore. All I knew was that I needed to get away from whatever that thing was."

He paused again, as if reliving the frantic drive down that lonely road. "The ambulance sped forward, and I kept my eyes fixed on the road, refusing to look back in the mirror. I do not know how long I drove like that, but it felt like an eternity."

Billa took a sip of his juice, the first since he had started telling the story. His hand shook slightly as he set the glass back down.

"When I finally reached the hospital in Kharar, I parked the ambulance and sat there for a few minutes, trying to make sense of what had just happened. My heart was pounding, and I could still hear the sound of her voice in my ears."

He looked at us with an expression that was both resigned and haunted. "To this day, I do not know what I saw or how she knew my name. All I know is that All I know is that the world is full of mysteries. And I never want to experience anything like that again."

For a moment, nobody spoke. The silence at our table was absolute, as if the weight of Billa's story had taken hold of all of us. The music and laughter from the wedding seemed far away, irrelevant in the face of what we had just heard.

Billa glanced at his watch, then stood up slowly. "I need to check on the arrangements," he said, his voice steady once again. "Enjoy the rest of the night, gentlemen."

With that, he gave us a nod and walked away, disappearing into the crowd.

We sat there in stunned silence, each of us lost in our thoughts. None of us dared to speak, as if breaking the silence would somehow bring the strange woman back into existence. Even the most skeptical among us looked shaken, their usual confidence replaced with quiet disbelief.

After Billa's story, it no longer mattered whether you believed in ghosts or not. The fear was real, and it had taken root in all of us. For a long time, nobody moved. We were physically present at the wedding, but our minds were far away, lost on that lonely road where the impossible had become real.

In the Mouth of Madness

The white-silver moonbeams bathed the horizon, casting a luminous glow that stretched across the vast fields, revealing every contour of the land. The far-reaching plains shimmered under the serene night, their scenic beauty unfolding like a painting untouched by time. A gentle breeze stirred the cornfields, making them sway lazily, their golden stalks glistening under the moon's soft gaze.

On the third-floor balcony at the rear of the college hostel, a young man leaned over the weathered parapet. Barely twenty, Raavi seemed lost in the depths of his thoughts, something quite uncharacteristic for someone known among his peers as carefree. Tonight, however, the weight of unspoken emotions anchored his usually buoyant spirit. Overhead, the sky stretched endlessly, a deep blue vault unmarred by clouds, typical of Punjab's tranquil autumn nights. The stars winked in scattered constellations, their light blending with the radiant moon that presided over the sprawling landscape.

From his vantage point, Raavi could see acres of farmland stretching into the night, segmented by rustic wooden fences and patches of wild shrubbery. A mosaic of fields lay beneath him, their orderly rows resembling the brushstrokes of a meticulous artist. The quiet hum of the night was occasionally punctuated by distant sounds. A creaking windmill, the rustling of dry leaves, and the faint murmur of laughter carried by the breeze added subtle life to the stillness.

Out of habit, he glanced toward the edge of the hostel courtyard, where a few familiar faces huddled together, their cigarettes glowing like tiny embers in the dark. They noticed him and waved lazily. Raavi lifted a hand in response, though his heart was not in it, and returned to his previous state of brooding, leaning heavily against the parapet.

The hostel belonged to an engineering college situated on the outskirts of Mohali, a city at the intersection of Punjab's urban sprawl and rural soul. Raavi had spent the evening trapped in a strange restlessness, unable to escape the cloud of doubt gathering over him. He skipped dinner, pacing his room without finding comfort, and now sought solace under the moon's gentle light, though his mind remained troubled.

He was halfway through his third semester, yet engineering felt like a cage, one forged from the expectations of others. The decision to pursue engineering had not

     THE OTHER SIDE OF HORIZON

been his own. Family pressure nudged him onto this path, dragging him further away from what his heart truly desired: journalism. His older brother followed the same route and now worked for a top firm, fulfilling the family's aspirations. For Raavi, however, the path felt hollow.

No matter how well he performed, and his recent exam results were proof of that, he felt uninspired and out of place. Every technical equation he solved seemed to take him further from the stories he longed to write and from the dreams he had shelved to meet expectations that were not his own.

There was one bright spot in his life, and that was his friends. Zorawar, Shally, and Avitej became the anchors that kept him afloat amid the monotony of engineering classes. Zorawar was the only one among them who stayed at home with his family, enjoying the comforts of a familiar environment. Shally and Avitej, a lively pair of twins from out of state, decided not to stay in the hostel. Instead, they rented a cozy apartment nearby. Their friendship gave Raavi the sense of belonging he lacked elsewhere, a reminder that not everything had to be endured alone.

The night deepened, and the stillness around him became almost hypnotic. Just as Raavi began to lose himself in thought again, an abrupt buzz shattered the quiet. The sound grated against his nerves, loud and intrusive, dragging him back into the moment.

Startled, he turned toward his room. It took only a moment to realize the source of the disturbance. His phone, buried somewhere amid the clutter on his desk, was vibrating insistently. With a groan, Raavi pushed away from the balcony and limped inside, still cursing his choice of ringtone. Its discordant, almost eerie tone seemed out of place in the calm night, grating on his nerves.

In his rush, his knee collided with the edge of the study table, sending a sharp sting through his leg. Wincing, he bit back a curse and rubbed the bruise absentmindedly as he fumbled for his phone. When he finally located it, his irritation melted into a small smile as Avitej's name appeared on the screen.

Avitej's text was characteristically brief but full of excitement:

"Dude, Zorawar bought a new SUV, and we are taking it for a test drive. We will reach the college in fifteen minutes. Be at the ATM near the college gate; we will pick you up there. We know it is late, but you can manage. Not calling since there is no balance."

Raavi shook his head, both amused and mildly annoyed. This was typical of Avitej, spontaneous and full of energy, never concerned with schedules or consequences. He glanced at the time and saw that it was already quarter past eleven. It was late, but the thought of a midnight adventure with his friends stirred something restless within him. Perhaps a drive beneath the stars would help shake off the heaviness that had settled in his chest.

The message brought a much-needed ray of light into Raavi's gloomy day. With newfound energy, he crossed to the built-in cupboard beside the entry door and flung it open. His clothes were in complete disarray, a mess reflecting how little he had cared to maintain things recently. He sifted through the pile hurriedly, looking for something suitable for the occasion. With a quick swipe, he pocketed the phone and grabbed his jacket from the back of the chair. As he made his way toward the door, a fleeting thought crossed his mind. What if he left it all behind? The college, the expectations, the constant tug-of-war between duty and dreams. The idea flickered briefly, tempting him with its simplicity, but it was gone as quickly as it came, slipping through his thoughts like sand between his fingers.

For now, there was only the promise of the open road, the hum of a new engine, and the laughter of friends who made him feel alive when everything else seemed uncertain.

And for tonight, that would be enough.

It took him only two minutes to read the message, and in ten minutes more, he was already at the gate chatting with the security guards.

College rules were strict. The final entry into the hostel was at 10 p.m., and anyone wanting to leave after that required special permission from the warden. It was well past 11 p.m., but that hardly mattered to Raavi. He had an arrangement with the security staff that worked to his advantage. On many occasions, he would bring them liquor and packed chicken as tokens of appreciation, a small investment that ensured they were always lenient with him. They were more than happy to make an exception tonight.

After a quick exchange of friendly banter with the guards, Raavi headed toward the ATM, located just a short walk from the college gate. As he reached the spot, a sudden realization hit him that he had forgotten his wallet in his rush; he sighed, mildly annoyed, but decided not to go back and instead sat down on the bench near the ATM, as instructed in the message.

It was one of those cold October nights that make you wish you had dressed warmer. The breeze was gentle, but it carried enough chill to cut through his light summer clothes, forcing him to tuck his hands into the pockets of his jeans for some warmth. He shifted in his seat, trying to get comfortable, though the cold made it difficult to sit still for long. With no other option, he leaned back and focused on the road, listening for the sound of an approaching vehicle.

His thoughts drifted again to the decision that had been tormenting him for weeks. The idea of discussing his passion for journalism with his family kept circling in his mind, but the uncertainty paralyzed him. Every time he considered raising the subject, a wall of doubt rose before him, blocking the words before they could form. He

   THE OTHER SIDE OF HORIZON

wondered if tonight's drive would offer him the clarity he sought, but even that hope felt distant.

Just as he closed his eyes to wander deeper into his thoughts, the sound of tires rolling over gravel caught his attention. The soft crunching grew louder, each shift in the gravel bringing the vehicle closer. From behind a blind curve, the white beams of headlights emerged, cutting through the darkness. As the vehicle rolled closer, the moonlight revealed it in full, a gleaming white Chevrolet Captiva, unmistakably new and built to impress.

The Captiva's sleek, muscular frame stood out, with its off-road design and powerful presence. Safari lights mounted on the roof added to its rugged charm, giving it the look of a beast ready to conquer any terrain. Raavi was impressed. As the headlights glared directly at him, he squinted and adjusted his path, walking around the front of the vehicle to avoid the blinding light.

The SUV looked even more majestic up close. It gave the impression of a small truck, embodying the perfect blend of elegance and strength. Raavi smiled and made his way to the back door, exchanging a friendly glance with the young men sitting in the front seats. As he opened the door, the warmth from inside greeted him like a welcome escape from the cold night.

He climbed in with a grin and shook hands with Zorawar and Avitej. Settling into his seat, he leaned forward, positioning himself between the front seats for an unblocked view of the road stretching ahead through the windshield.

"You are late," Raavi said with mock indignation. "I almost froze to death out here."

Zorawar burst into laughter. "If we had known, we would have come an hour later just for the fun of it," he said, grinning.

Raavi chuckled, the camaraderie lifting his spirits. His initial annoyance vanished as he admired the vehicle's plush interiors. Every detail spoke of luxury. The seats were crafted from soft leather, with adjustable headrests for added comfort. A sunroof stretched above, hinting at endless possibilities for future road trips. The gear knob and steering wheel were wrapped in smooth leather, adding a touch of sophistication to the already impressive cabin.

"Congratulations on the new beast, Zorawar," Raavi said sincerely, giving the interior an approving glance.

Zorawar nodded with pride. "Thanks, man. Thought it was time for an upgrade."

With a smooth turn of the steering wheel, Zorawar maneuvered the SUV out of the parking spot. In just a couple of minutes, they were on the open highway, cruising effortlessly at 100 kilometers an hour. The road stretched ahead like an endless ribbon under the moonlight, and Zorawar's love for driving became evident with every smooth turn and acceleration.

He reached for the radio and began switching stations, searching for one with decent reception. A dull, melancholic tune came through the speakers, but Zorawar frowned and moved on. The next station offered static, and the one after that played a commercial jingle. Finally, he found something to his liking, an upbeat song that perfectly matched the mood of the night.

For a while, the car was filled with laughter and lighthearted chatter. They joked about the most trivial things, each moment wrapped in the warmth of friendship. Eventually, the conversation faded, replaced by the comforting silence that only close friends can share.

There was something about the night that words could not capture. The synergy of the cold air, the faint music from the radio, and the quiet companionship created an atmosphere that felt almost magical. The usual chaos of life seemed far away, replaced by a sense of peace none of them had expected to find.

The road was empty, save for the occasional vehicle passing by in the opposite direction. Even the nocturnal creatures seemed to have retreated to their shelters, unwilling to brave the sudden drop in temperature. The SUV's engine hummed steadily, blending with the soft melodies from the radio. In that moment, everything felt right. It was the kind of night that stays with you, etched into memory not because of any grand event, but because of the quiet beauty found in its simplicity.

Raavi leaned back, closing his eyes for a brief moment. The cold no longer bothered him. In the company of his friends, on this tranquil highway under the starlit sky, the weight of his worries seemed lighter. For now, the questions about his future could wait. All that mattered was the open road ahead, the music, and the comfort of knowing he was exactly where he needed to be.

They sat in silence, letting the music and the cool October night weave a gentle spell over them. The hum of the engine faded into the background as they enjoyed the moment. The air was crisp, carrying with it the faint scent of dew settling on the fields beyond the highway. It was a rare kind of silence, the kind that felt natural and comforting, as if words would only disrupt the harmony they had found. For a while, none of them felt the need to speak, content to simply exist in the peace of the night.

Avitej finally broke the silence when he noticed a petrol pump up ahead, accompanied by a small tea stall nestled beside it. Checking his watch, he realized that nearly an hour had passed since they first set off. They pulled into the station, filled up the tank, and decided to stop by the tea stall for a quick break.

The tea stall was small, run by an old man with tired eyes and slow movements, catering mostly to truckers passing through on long night journeys. Three or four worn-out benches were scattered haphazardly in front of the stall, their faded wood telling stories of countless travelers who had rested there. At the center of the makeshift seating arrangement, a small fire crackled and burned brightly, providing warmth against the chill that hung in the air.

As they sat by the fire, the heat seeped into their bodies, soothing them in a way that made them feel lighter. Each of them carried unspoken burdens that had weighed them down. Raavi, though usually easygoing, had been consumed by his recent dilemma about his future, the tug-of-war between his passion for journalism and his family's expectations. Avitej, always anxious about his poor grades, struggled with the constant pressure from his nervous mother, who feared for his academic performance. Zorawar, despite his cheerful demeanor, often found himself lost in memories of his late parents, their absence leaving a quiet ache in his heart.

For the next hour, they sat by the fire, sipping hot tea and munching on biscuits. The warmth of the tea mixed with the comfort of their shared presence, easing the weight of their troubles. They gazed into the flickering flames, their thoughts drifting as if carried by the fire's glow. For a little while, they forgot about their responsibilities and the worries that haunted them. In that moment, it felt as if time had slowed, allowing them to simply be. The fire, the tea, and the chilly night provided a kind of solace none of them had expected to find.

Eventually, the time came to leave. None of them wanted to step away from the perfect stillness they had discovered, reluctant to leave the comforting trance that surrounded them. Yet, with a shared sigh, they climbed back into the SUV, ready for the next leg of their journey. Zorwar took the driver's seat, Avitej took the front passenger seat, and Raavi had no choice but to sit in the back.Zorawar switched on the radio once again, scanning the frequencies for a local station that could fill the quiet with music. The engine hummed back to life as they pulled out into the cool night air. The highway stretched before them, shrouded in mist and silence, with only the occasional glimmer of passing headlights in the distance.

They were making their way back toward the college, the road smooth beneath the tires, when Zorawar abruptly slowed the vehicle and brought it to a halt. The sudden stop jolted everyone out of their quiet reverie.

"Oh damn, do you think we should test the off-road capability of this beast?" Zorawar asked, glancing at his friends with a mischievous grin.

"As you wish, Michael Schumacher," Raavi replied, his sarcasm cutting through the silence like a knife.

"There are supposed to be some trails around here that lead to small villages," Avitej began cautiously, "but I do not think it is a good idea to….."

"Look out, you fellows!" Zorawar interrupted, steering the SUV sharply toward a narrow trail that branched off from the highway.

The moment the vehicle left the highway and entered the trail, the atmosphere shifted. The path was muddy and uneven, flanked by towering trees on both sides. The narrow entrance gave way to a confined stretch that did not widen at any point, requiring Zorawar to drive slowly and with meticulous care. With only two feet of space on either side of the SUV, every movement of the steering wheel demanded precision.

The further they went, the more unsettling the trail became. It was well-trodden but strangely deserted, with no signs of life in sight. Not a single house or light flickered in the distance. The dense canopy of trees above them blocked out the moon and stars, plunging the trail into an unnatural darkness. The comforting glow of the moon, which had been their companion earlier, was nowhere to be found.

As they ventured deeper, the night that had once felt serene and magical now seemed eerie and oppressive. The air grew colder, and small patches of fog drifted across the trail. They floated low and thin, resembling wisps of smoke, though they vanished quickly with the SUV's movement. The silence that had once felt peaceful now weighed on them, thick and stifling.

Raavi shifted in his seat, unease spreading through him. "This place feels strange," he muttered, glancing out the window.

Zorawar's hands tightened on the steering wheel, his usual confidence waning slightly. "It is probably just the fog," he said, though the uncertainty in his voice did not go unnoticed.

As the SUV crawled along the narrow path, the lively banter from earlier faded into anxious silence. They had set out to test the off-road prowess of the new vehicle, but now the excitement had evaporated, replaced by a growing sense of dread. Every twist and turn in the trail seemed to pull them further into the unknown, and the further they drove, the more they felt like intruders in a place that did not welcome them.

There was something deeply unsettling about the trail. The darkness felt heavier here, as if it carried secrets they were not meant to uncover. The absence of the moonlight made it difficult to judge their surroundings, and the suffocating stillness gave the impression that the world outside the trail no longer existed. Even the trees seemed to lean closer, their branches twisting and reaching like silent observers.

An ominous feeling settled over them, creeping into their minds like a shadow. The mist swirled around the tires, and the road ahead stretched endlessly, showing no signs of opening into a village or connecting back to the highway. Each of them felt an inexplicable sense of impending doom, as though they were being drawn toward something they could neither see nor understand.

Raavi looked toward Zorawar, hoping for reassurance, but Zorawar's focused expression gave little comfort. Avitej sat stiffly in the back seat, staring out into the darkness with wide eyes. None of them spoke, each lost in their own unease. The night had taken on a life of its own, shifting from a quiet escape into something far more sinister.

They continued along the trail, tension filling the silence between them. With every passing moment, the unsettling feeling grew stronger, wrapping around them like a cloak. The adventure they had set out on now felt like a mistake, but there was no turning back. The trail demanded they see it through, and they could only hope that whatever lay ahead would not be as ominous as the darkness that surrounded them.

"Hell with this silence, I cannot take it anymore. I have been on this trail before. We will get out soon, damn it. I could not even cross eighty on this godforsaken road," Zorawar said, a smile tugging at the corners of his lips.

His voice carried an odd, lilting tone, almost as if he were reciting lyrics from a song. The smile was intended to reassure, but it only added to the discomfort in the car. It seemed too casual, as though he were pretending that everything was fine when nothing felt right. Without looking at his friends, Zorawar reached forward and turned up the radio, filling the cabin with music that now felt out of place.

Avitej sat perfectly still in the front seat, the only one wearing his seatbelt. He kept his hands folded tightly in his lap, occasionally tapping his fingers to the beat of the radio. His posture was rigid, as if bracing for something unseen. In the back seat, Raavi shifted uncomfortably, glancing at Zorawar. There was something unsettling about how relaxed he seemed, one hand draped lazily over the steering wheel. It was as though he was using the wheel to prop himself up, pretending to be at ease when it was obvious he was not.

The night grew colder with every passing moment, and Raavi shivered as the chill crept through his thin clothes. He opened his mouth to ask Zorawar to turn on the heater, but before he could speak, the radio crackled, losing its signal. Zorawar twisted the knob, switching between stations, but all they heard was harsh static echoing through the speakers.

He paused for a moment, hoping the signal would clear, but the static persisted. He pressed the power button repeatedly, but the radio refused to shut off. The controls were completely unresponsive, a strange malfunction given that Zorawar had bought the car just yesterday. Bewildered, Zorawar tried everything to turn off the sound, but the radio seemed to have a mind of its own.

Before any of them could comprehend the strange malfunction, an old man appeared in the middle of the road, not more than twenty meters ahead. He emerged out

   THE OTHER SIDE OF HORIZON

of nowhere, as though conjured from the mist that clung to the edges of the trail. Zorawar cursed under his breath and yanked the wheel, but with the narrow path, the car's speed, and his divided attention, it was impossible to stop in time.

The SUV hurtled forward, the metallic bumper aimed directly at the old man. Both Zorawar and Avitej shut their eyes instinctively, bracing for the inevitable impact. Yet, there was no jolt, no thud, no sign of a collision. The only sound was the screech of the tires as the SUV skidded to a halt on the muddy trail.

Zorawar's voice broke through the tense silence, trembling with disbelief. "In God's name, what have I done? Come on, let's check. I hope he is not dead."

Before Zorawar could open the door, Raavi's voice, sharp and urgent, cut through the night.

"Go. Let's go, Zorawar!" Raavi's hand shot up, pointing in the direction opposite to where the old man had stood. His voice carried a sense of desperation, unlike anything his friends had heard from him before.

Something in Raavi's tone sent a chill down Zorawar's spine. Without a word, he slammed the gear into drive and pressed the accelerator. The SUV roared to life, tearing down the path in the direction Raavi had indicated. Zorawar stole a quick glance at Avitej, as if seeking validation, but Avitej sat with his head bowed, his hands pressed against his forehead as though lost in deep thought.

Zorawar slowed the car and finally brought it to a halt a few minutes later, turning off the engine with a shaky hand. The silence returned, heavier than before, wrapping around them like a thick fog. He turned to Raavi, confusion and frustration evident on his face.

"What was that? Maybe the old man is not dead. We could still help him. Why did you want to leave?" Zorawar asked, his voice filled with disbelief and a tinge of shame.

Raavi sat motionless, his face pale and drawn. The recent events had clearly rattled him. His hands shook as he gripped the edge of his seat, and his breathing was shallow and uneven, as though he was struggling to steady himself.

He took a deep breath, trying to sound composed, but his voice wavered. "Believe me when I say this. It is in our best interest to leave now."

Zorawar stared at him, baffled by the uncharacteristic fear in his friend's voice. Raavi was usually the carefree one, the one who never seemed fazed by anything. But tonight, he looked like someone who had seen something far beyond their understanding. The chill in his voice, the fear in his eyes was unlike anything Zorawar had ever witnessed in him before.

Zorawar exchanged a glance with Avitej, who remained eerily silent, his forehead still resting in his hands. Something had shifted among them, something far beyond the ordinary. The strange encounter on the trail, the malfunctioning radio, and Raavi's inexplicable fear had changed the tone of the night entirely.

Zorawar brought the car to halt, ready to tur back. but as his hand hovered near the handle, he glanced into the rear-view mirror, intending to catch one last glimpse of his frightened friend in the back seat. But then something shifted within him, a feeling so strong it was impossible to ignore. His heart raced. In an instant, he changed his mind, putting the keys back into the ignition. The SUV roared to life with a low rumble, and without a word, Zorawar sped away, the tires kicking up gravel as they left the eerie trail behind.

Avitej stared at Zorawar, his expression frozen in disbelief. He tried to make sense of Zorawar's sudden change of heart, but the fear that gripped him made it impossible to focus. For a fleeting moment, it felt as though his body was not even there, as if he was a fragment of air, floating aimlessly inside the car. The silence that followed was suffocating. No one spoke, and the chill inside the vehicle deepened, wrapping around them like an invisible fog.

Zorawar drove in tense silence, his eyes flickering constantly to the rear-view mirror, more often than usual. Ten minutes passed, each one dragging on as they approached a clearing up ahead. At the end of the trail stood a large, weather-beaten wooden board cemented into the ground. The board was so old that whatever had once been written on it had long faded away, leaving only cracked and splintered wood behind. The SUV rolled forward, finally emerging from the dense forest onto the smooth surface of the highway.

The moment the tires touched the asphalt, the radio came back to life, its static replaced by a clear tune that filled the cabin. Zorawar exhaled deeply, stealing another glance at the rear-view mirror. Seeing nothing unusual, he sighed with relief, and Raavi did the same, the tension in his face softening just slightly. Zorawar turned his head toward Raavi, giving him a reassuring nod, though the unease still lingered between them.

Avitej, still shaken, wanted to ask the questions that swirled in his mind, but before he could speak, Zorawar broke the silence.

"How did you know, Raavi?" Zorawar asked quietly, keeping his gaze on the road ahead but glancing briefly at Raavi through the mirror.

Avitej exchanged puzzled looks with Zorawar, feeling as if he had missed some vital piece of the puzzle. It was like being a student thrust into an advanced thermodynamics class with no prior knowledge. His heart raced as he wondered what his friends had seen that he had not.

Raavi's voice, though unsteady, carried a haunting weight. His hands trembled, and his legs quivered beneath the residual chill still clinging to him. "I did not close my eyes like the two of you did," he said, his voice faltering. "I saw it happen, and we never hit that man. Our vehicle passed straight through him as if he was not real. I watched him dissolve into smoke right in front of me. And then... then I felt it."

He paused, struggling to steady his breath. "The temperature dropped, and I knew there was someone else in the car, sitting right next to me. I felt it, as clear as day. It was as if I was being buried alive. The pressure, the presence... I knew we had to leave."

Zorawar listened silently, his face pale and drawn, as if reliving the moment all over again. He took a breath, gathering his thoughts before speaking. "When I was about to turn back the car, I looked in the rear-view mirror to check on you," he began, his voice low and filled with unease. "And that is when I saw him."

Both Raavi and Avitej leaned in slightly, their hearts pounding in anticipation.

"He had a fair face, and the grin on it was so wide that his eyes became slits," Zorawar continued, his voice barely above a whisper. "When I looked at him through the mirror, it felt like I was staring off into a place that should not exist. He sat there, right beside you, as clear as I see you now. And he stayed in the car until we left that trail. The moment we hit the highway and the radio started working again, he was gone."

A heavy silence settled over the car, each of them lost in their thoughts. Avitej's chest tightened, his heart pounding against his ribcage as if it would burst at any moment. He clutched his chest, trying to steady himself, overwhelmed by the realization of what they had just escaped. For the first time in his life, he felt truly grateful to be alive.

They drove down that highway many times after that night, hoping to find the eerie trail again, but it was as if the path had never existed. No sign of it could be found, no narrow entrance between the trees, and no worn wooden board marking the way. It was as if the entire experience had been a fleeting nightmare, vanishing into thin air the moment it ended.

But none of them ever forgot. The memory of that cold, silent night lingered, a dark shadow that followed them quietly, always just out of reach but never truly gone.

And though they tried to move on, none of them could shake the feeling that somewhere out there, beneath the cover of mist and shadow, the old man with the wide grin was still waiting.

The Meeting

It had been seven long years since I left India. Moving abroad had been like shedding a heavy, suffocating skin, and now, returning to the place I had abandoned felt strange, almost unnatural. The very name of the place stirred a deep, aching nostalgia within me. After all, I had spent the first eighteen years of my life here, surrounded by memories both bitter and sweet. India, however, had not been kind. During my time here, I had experienced tragedies that left scars too deep to heal. I lost my entire family in a devastating accident, and not long after, my uncle, who had been like a second father to me, passed away unexpectedly, marking the final chapter of my life in India.

Grief-stricken and weary of the people around me, I severed all ties with my relatives. Their narrow-mindedness and self-centered nature made it easy for me to walk away without a second thought. To them, I no longer existed, and they were dead to me as well. For seven years, I never contacted any of them, and they never reached out.

I promised myself that I would never return to Punjab, my hometown, until now. This time, my return was not personal. It was professional.

I had become a writer for a publishing company abroad, and an unusual opportunity had fallen into my lap: a short story assignment on a series of unsolved murders that had taken place in Punjab a few months earlier. This was my first overseas project, a career-defining chance that few young writers were fortunate enough to receive. It was not just an assignment; it was a stepping stone toward everything I had worked so hard for.

The assignment was scheduled to last fifteen days, but from the very start, the visit felt like an extension of the misfortunes I had left behind. Despite my excitement, the first fourteen days passed without any meaningful progress. I worked tirelessly, determined to uncover something substantial, but the trail of the unsolved murders remained cold. No evidence. No revelations. The police had no suspects, and the killer had vanished without a trace.

I had done everything in my power to make sense of the case. I met with the families of the deceased, interviewed locals who were familiar with the events, and visited the road where the murders had taken place multiple times. I even sought assistance from police officials, hoping to gain access to anything that might have been overlooked. Yet, every lead ended in frustration. The story was slipping through my fingers, and my dream of making a strong debut on this overseas project seemed destined for failure.

Here is a summary of what I managed to gather about the case:

"The site of the murders was an abandoned road, bordered by a canal on one side and dense trees on the other. The road had fallen into disuse after a newer, wider highway was constructed parallel to it. Aside from a newly built temple that seemed to have been added after the events, the road was empty and isolated. Its desolation made it a prime hunting ground for someone with sinister intentions. The combination of the secluded location, the canal, and the trees offered an ideal environment for a predator who could strike unseen and vanish without leaving a trail.

What stood out among the incidents was the last case, which finally brought the series of murders into the public eye. Two young men in their mid-twenties were found dead, and a girl, by some miracle, had survived. Her survival was the sole reason the massacre had come to light. Until that point, the missing persons reports had gone unnoticed, and the abandoned vehicles found along the roadside had not raised any red flags. It was only after the girl gave her testimony that the authorities realized the full extent of the tragedy.

Following her statement, the police decided to halt the flow of the canal and search it thoroughly. What they found shocked them to the core. The bodies of the two boys from the last incident were recovered from the canal, but they were not alone. As the search continued, body after body was pulled from the water, each one lodged against the bars beneath a small bridge downstream. In total, ten bodies were recovered.

The realization that all the victims had been male added a chilling dimension to the case. The post-mortem reports revealed no traces of sedatives or drugs, which made the deaths even more baffling. Each death was attributed to hypoxia—suffocation due to a lack of oxygen in the brain—consistent with drowning. One of the victims from the final incident had been a promising boxer, well-known for his athletic prowess and swimming skills. How someone of his physical strength and ability had drowned without any evidence of foul play remained a mystery that no one could explain.

The most important piece of the puzzle lay with the girl who had survived, but accessing her was no easy task. Her mental state had deteriorated following the incident, and she was placed under professional psychiatric care. Her identity was kept confidential, and despite my

 THE OTHER SIDE OF HORIZON

best efforts, both legal and otherwise, all I could uncover was her last name: Brar."

The more I learned, the more the story felt like it was slipping through my grasp. Each piece of information I gathered mirrored what was already available online, leaving me frustrated and defeated. My ambitious plan to craft a groundbreaking story seemed destined to crumble, as the unsolved murders remained just that—unsolved.

With only one day left on my trip, I stood at the edge of failure, my dreams of launching a spectacular overseas project hanging by a thread.

It was the evening of the thirteenth day that I gave up on the project, resigning myself to the fact that I had failed to find any significant breakthrough. Frustrated and exhausted, I accepted defeat. I decided to spend my last day and a half in peace, hoping to unwind before returning to my hectic life in Canada.

I began with a visit to a local terrace restaurant, known for its food and serene ambience. The night was perfect, late March, with a cool spring breeze in the air. The stars shone brilliantly, scattered across a sky so clear it seemed unreal. From the seventh-floor terrace, the view was breathtaking. Below, the city sparkled with lights, flickering like stars against the night. The moon bathed the terrace in its silver glow, casting a soft light on the people around me. Everything felt peaceful, a fleeting moment of tranquility after the turmoil of the past days.

Seated in a corner, I let the night's beauty wash over me. For a long while, I gazed in silence at the shimmering skyline, lost in the serenity that surrounded me. It felt like a welcome escape, a reminder of a simpler time. The waiter's polite cough brought me back to reality. He handed me the menu with a smile and stepped away, leaving me to my thoughts.

As I flipped through the menu, I saw her. She sat not far from me, and the sight of her took my breath away. Her cheeks glowed like the petals of a red rose, her hair flowed as dark as the clouds before a storm, and her eyes sparkled like the brightest stars in the night sky. When she smiled, it felt like a soothing balm for a weary soul, like rain on parched earth. A strange feeling gripped me the moment I saw her, as if her face held a significance I could not yet grasp.

I sat in silence, trying to make sense of the feeling, but it only deepened. Something about her seemed familiar, as though we had crossed paths before. Just as I drifted deeper into my thoughts, the waiter returned, apologizing for the interruption and ready to take my order. Startled, I placed my order hastily and turned back toward her table, only to find it empty. The waiter was already clearing away the dishes, the chairs now vacant.

A pang of disappointment hit me. I scanned the terrace, hoping to catch a glimpse of her before she disappeared entirely. My eyes lingered on the exit, but she was gone.

It was not only her beauty that unsettled me but also the nagging feeling that I knew her, though I could not place when or where. The more I tried to recall, the stronger the feeling became, but no answer came to mind.

The meal was delicious, and the night sky remained as captivating as before, but my thoughts were consumed by the mysterious girl. Unable to focus, I left the restaurant feeling restless and returned to my hotel, hoping sleep would bring some clarity. That night, I lay awake, haunted by the strange familiarity of her face.

The next day, my final one in India, arrived too soon. My flight was scheduled for the following morning, leaving me little time to wrap up any remaining tasks. I woke early and completed the formalities needed before departure. As a final gesture, I revisited the road where the murders had occurred and stepped inside the newly built temple nearby. I had noticed the temple on my first visit to the area but had not taken the time to explore it until now. Stepping inside felt oddly comforting, like reconnecting with a part of myself that had been lost for years.

After returning to my hotel, I spent the afternoon exploring the market. It was there, amidst the bustling crowds and colorful stalls, that I saw her again. She walked with a group of girls her age, her laughter ringing out like a melody that made my heart race. I could hardly believe my luck, seeing her twice in such a short span of time. It felt like a chance not to be missed.

I slipped on my dark shades, grateful for the cover they provided, and followed her discreetly. I kept a few steps behind, determined to uncover the connection I felt without drawing attention to myself. As I walked beside her, memories began to surface, stirring like ripples in a still pond.

Then, all at once, it became clear. Her name was Reet, and she had been a part of my life long ago. Our families had been close, with business ties that kept us connected. We had attended the same school, and I often saw her at family gatherings and school events. Even back then, Reet had been admired for her beauty and intelligence. However, her sharp attitude had earned her a reputation among our peers, and many considered her aloof. But to me, she had always been kind.

The memories flooded back, vivid and undeniable. I remembered how she stood by me during the most difficult time of my life, the year I lost my parents. When everyone else distanced themselves, she stayed. Day after day, she joined me during lunch breaks, even when I barely spoke. Some days, she would bring me lunch, offering comfort through her presence when words could not reach me.

I had not appreciated her kindness back then. Consumed by grief, I pushed everyone away, including her. But she never gave up on me, staying by my side until my final exams. Looking back, I realized how much her presence had meant. It was a lifeline I had not recognized at the time, and the weight of that realization hit me hard.

As I walked beside her, the guilt that had gnawed at me for years resurfaced. I had left India without so much as a goodbye, cutting ties with everyone, including Reet. It was an act of selfishness, born out of my desire to escape the pain. Now, seeing her again after all these years, I wanted nothing more than to thank her for what she had done. But I hesitated.

She gave no sign of recognizing me, and I wondered if it was too late to bridge the gap between us. Or perhaps the real reason I held back was the guilt I carried for leaving without a word. I had been weak back then, running away instead of facing my grief.

Now, standing in the busy market, I knew I could not carry this burden any longer. The crack that had formed in my heart all those years ago needed to be mended. And the only way to do that was to find the courage to confront the past.

I knew I had to thank Reet for everything she had done and apologize for my selfish behavior. In that moment, I made a sudden resolve. I would go and speak to her. I was certain that, by bringing up some old memories, she would remember me. Her two friends walking alongside her complicated the situation slightly, but I summoned the courage to approach.

I called her name in the same familiar way I had used all those years ago. Her steps came to an abrupt halt, and her friends stopped beside her, exchanging curious glances. She turned her head toward me, her expression puzzled and bemused. I was about to introduce myself, ready to remind her of our shared past, when something unexpected caught my attention. A small droplet glistened on her cheek. At first, I thought it was a drop of water, but then it dawned on me that it was a tear.

I stood there, frozen in place, trying to make sense of it. Before I could say a word, Reet took two quick steps toward me and embraced me warmly. Her sudden gesture left me stunned. Not only had she remembered me, but she also showed no sign of resentment, even after the way I had abandoned her without a word.

Her friends, surprised by the sudden turn of events, asked if everything was all right, but Reet paid them no mind. Her voice, soft yet heavy with emotion, reached my ears as she spoke.

"It has been ages, Sam. Where have you been all this time?"

Hearing her voice again felt like a balm on my weary heart. Overwhelmed by her kindness, I hugged her back, though guilt weighed heavily on my mind. Remembering how I used to talk to her about my dream of becoming an astronomer, I answered with a nostalgic smile.

"Moon, where else?"

She laughed, recognizing the joke, and the sound of her laughter made my heart feel lighter. She wiped away her tears and smiled, a smile that had not changed despite all the years that had passed. It was the same innocent smile that I had cherished since we were children. Seeing it again stirred a deep nostalgia within me, and my heart grew heavy with the flood of memories that came rushing back.

"I have missed you so much, Sam," she said, holding my hand tightly. She introduced me to her friends with enthusiasm, giving me the kind of warm, unfiltered introduction that only Reet could provide.

I stood there, listening with a smile as she spoke about me. Her words flowed effortlessly, just as they used to when we were younger. It felt surreal, as if I were caught in a dream I never wanted to end. The evening sun dipped lower, casting long shadows over the streets, and the sky began to darken. I felt like I had stepped into a moment outside of time, one I wished would never slip away.

Reet continued chatting, making plans for the next day. She mentioned how much she wanted to catch up properly and talk about everything we had missed. She even brought up how happy her father would be to see me again. Yet, as she spoke, her excitement only deepened the ache inside me.

I had kept my departure a secret, but I knew I could not let her plan in vain. As much as it pained me, I had to tell her the truth. My flight was scheduled for the next morning, and I would be gone before the sun rose.

Reet noticed the sadness in my expression. "What is wrong?" she asked, her voice laced with concern.

I knew I had to tell her now, though the words felt heavy on my tongue. Gathering all the courage I could muster, I looked into her eyes and spoke the truth.

"Reet, I am leaving tomorrow morning."

Her face fell, the joy draining from her features, replaced by a look of quiet disappointment. I braced myself for what might follow, but before I could say anything more, she turned to her friends and asked for their leave. They smiled, shook my hand politely, and left without hesitation.

When Reet turned back to me, her expression had softened. A smile played on her lips as she spoke with a gentle, almost playful tone.

"We have little time then. Let us grab something to eat. My treat."

Once again, Reet showed me the kindness and grace that I had long forgotten. Without hesitation, she led me to a nearby restaurant she had always loved, boasting about the delicious food it served. True to her word, the food exceeded my expectations. The traditional flavors reminded me of simpler times, and every bite felt like a journey back to the past.

As we ate, we delved into the stories of our childhood, recalling the moments we had shared when life was easier and everything felt perfect. One story after another surfaced, each one bringing laughter that felt unburdened by the years that had passed. In those moments, we were children again, free from the worries of adulthood.

The memories I had buried deep within my heart began to emerge, one by one. It felt brilliant, like rediscovering treasures I had thought were lost. I realized then that these memories were not burdens to hide but gifts to cherish. They were a part of me, and it was time to embrace them.

As the night deepened, I knew there was one thing left to say, something I had carried with me for years. The guilt of how I had left her weighed heavily on my conscience, and it was time to let it go.

"You remember that winter, when my parents passed away?" I asked, my voice heavy with emotion.

Reet nodded, her expression softening as she recalled those difficult days.

I took a deep breath, ready to finally say what had been locked inside me for so long. "Back then, I was lost. I shut everyone out, even you, and I never got to tell you how much your kindness meant to me. You stayed by my side when no one else did, and I did not appreciate it at the time. I was selfish, Reet, and I am sorry for leaving without saying goodbye and not contacting you in all these years."

Her eyes shimmered with understanding, and for a moment, the silence between us said more than any words could. I had carried the weight of that regret for far too long, and now, with those words spoken, I felt the crack in my heart begin to mend.

Reet's expression shifted, and the lively spark that had animated her face moments ago faded into something sorrowful. She nodded in response, though no words accompanied the gesture. The silence felt heavy between us, so I decided to break it, speaking from the heart.

"Those were the hardest days of my life," I began, my voice steady but full of emotion. "I want to thank you for everything, for all that you did back then. I tried to act brave, pretending that everything was fine, but it was not. My heart was breaking from the inside, and I was slowly giving up hope. I felt myself slipping, losing the will to fight. It was your presence during that time that kept me going, keeping me from falling into darkness. I could have ended up lost, like so many others who turn to drugs to escape. But you stayed with me, and it made all the difference."

I paused, feeling the weight of my guilt. "And despite everything you did for me, I left without so much as a goodbye or even a phone call. It was selfish of me, and I have regretted that decision ever since. I wished, for years, that I could take it back. Now that we are here, I just wanted to say—"

Before I could finish, Reet interrupted me. Her eyes, glistening with unshed tears, locked with mine as she held my hand tightly.

"You remember how I struggled to fit in at school? How they made fun of me for not having friends? All the harsh words, the taunts—they never really bothered me because I had you. You were my only friend, and that was all I needed to be happy," she said, her voice filled with emotion. "I was afraid of losing you, Sam. I stayed by your side back then not just for you, but for myself too. I was selfish, in my own way."

A strange sensation spread through me, welling up from deep within. I blinked, trying to understand what I was feeling, and then I realized that I was crying. Silent tears blurred my vision as the emotions I had buried for so long surfaced all at once.

Reet's expression softened, and with a playful smile, she tried to cheer me up. "What has happened to you, Sammy? I have never seen you cry before. And this is the first time you have thanked me for anything and it feels so odd. You have changed a lot."

We sat back in our chairs, lulled by the weight of our shared memories and the peaceful night sky above. Neither of us spoke for a while, content to sip our coffee in silence. The cool night breeze began to pick up, and Reet pulled her shawl closer around her shoulders.

Breaking the quiet, she asked, "What is this project of yours that brought you back here?"

I told her everything amd how important the project was to me, how I had hoped it would be my big break, and how I had spent days chasing a story only to come up empty-handed. I mentioned the one clue I had uncovered: the girl's last name, Brar.

Reet listened without interruption, but as I finished speaking, I noticed a change in her expression. She sat quietly, staring at the moon, lost in thought. Her silence stretched for several moments before she finally turned to me, her voice heavy with sadness.

"I feel sorry for all the bad experiences you have had in India," she said. "It has been a painful place for you, and I understand why you never wanted to come back. In the end, it seems this trip went exactly as you expected, and it gave you no reason to think otherwise."

Her words caught me off guard. For a moment, I could only look at her, lost in the depth of her gaze. Then, with a small smile, I spoke softly.

"You are wrong, Reet. I got to meet you, and that means more to me than the project ever could. Who says the trip was not a success? Meeting you made it a great success, and I could not have asked for a better outcome. This trip has helped me leave behind all the bad memories I carried with me. And I promise you, Reet, I am looking forward to visiting India again just to meet you."

     THE OTHER SIDE OF HORIZON

Her somber eyes lit up, and a radiant smile spread across her face. She looked like a child who had just been given a bigger ice cream to replace the one that had fallen from her hand. There was a sense of peace and satisfaction in her expression as she glanced toward the night sky.

"You remember how much I loved to write?" she asked, her voice light with nostalgia. "Since you could not find a story, it is only right that I help you with one. Let me tell you my version of what happened with the girl on that road. I think it will cheer you up."

Reet took a deep breath and began her narration, her voice soft and thoughtful, as though she was speaking only to herself. I leaned in, listening closely, a smile lingering on my face as she wove her tale.

"It is a little unrealistic, but please bear with me," she said in a low tone. "That night, the two boys and the girl, Brar came out of the movie theatre and stopped by a roadside stall to grab a quick snack. It had rained earlier in the evening, cooling the air and offering everyone some relief from the heat. The streets were still wet, and the moon peeked from behind heavy clouds, casting a faint silver glow on the puddles that dotted the ground."

Her voice grew quieter, as if the story were playing out before her eyes.

"Everything began, just like in the movies. While they ate, the mischievous boy, the son of a prominent politician, decided to stir things up. He mentioned the rising number of missing person reports in the area, a story he had picked up from his father's security officer. He challenged the others to visit the deserted area near the canal at this late hour, calling it an adventure."

I could almost see the scene unfolding as she spoke. Reet's storytelling was vivid and rich, her words painting a picture of the fateful night.

"The girl, Brar, disapproved immediately. She was exhausted and wanted to go home, but her cousin, the brave boy, a state-level boxer accepted the challenge. His competitive spirit got the better of him, as if he needed to prove his courage. Brar argued with her cousin, trying to persuade him to let it go, but the mischievous boy had already set the trap. He knew exactly how to play with his friend's ego. With his pride at stake, the brave boy refused to back down."

Reet paused briefly, a wistful look crossing her face before she continued. "Brar could not leave her cousin to go alone, so, reluctantly, she decided to join them. And just like that, the three of them were off, heading toward the infamous road, unaware of the nightmare awaiting them.

"The night was dark, and pools of water glistened on the road from the rain earlier that evening. The cool breeze made the air feel crisp, and the clouds shifted just enough for the moon to make fleeting appearances. Mischievous boy, now driving, sang ridiculous songs in odd tones, making Brar roll her eyes in exasperation. Meanwhile, the brave boy sat beside him, smiling at his friend's antics.

"Brar sat in the back, pressing her forehead against the cold window, watching the silver wilderness stretch endlessly into the dark. The wind whistled softly as the car sped along the narrow road, and she felt silly for coming along on this pointless trip. Yet, deep down, she could not shake the feeling that something was wrong, that this was not just another harmless dare."

Reet's tone grew heavier, her words casting a shadow over the story. "When they finally reached the abandoned road, the atmosphere changed. The place reeked of foreboding, as though it had witnessed things no human should ever see. For a moment, the car fell into silence, and each of them felt the oppressive weight of the eerie aura surrounding them.

"And then, as if on cue, the car sputtered and stalled in the middle of the deserted road. No matter how many times the mischievous boy turned the key, the engine refused to start again. It was all playing out like the perfect scene from a horror film."

She leaned forward slightly, her voice dropping to a near whisper. "The mischievous boy tried to laugh it off, mocking Brar with strange noises, but it was clear that he too was unnerved by the car's sudden failure. The two boys got out to investigate, opening the bonnet to inspect the engine. They joked nervously, pretending to be unfazed, but Brar could tell they were unsettled."

I listened intently as Reet's story darkened.

"Brar stayed inside the car, uneasy and on edge. She scanned the area through the windows, her eyes following the patches of moonlight that pierced through the dense clouds. Every shadow seemed to shift, and every breeze whispered warnings. She wanted to get out, but her cousin had told her to stay put. Reluctantly, she obeyed, her anxiety growing with every passing second.

"As the two boys fussed over the engine, Brar heard the mischievous boy announce that he was going to relieve himself by the canal. She watched him amble toward the canal's edge, his silhouette fading into the darkness. Before he disappeared entirely, the brave boy called out to him in a mocking tone.

"'Beware of the dark,' he warned sarcastically, 'for no one knows what dwells in it.'"

Reet's voice lingered on those words, filling the air between us with a sense of dread. I felt myself drawn deeper into the story, as if I too were sitting in that car, staring into the darkness, waiting for something to happen.

"The mischievous boy whistled cheerfully as he strolled toward the canal, paying no attention to the brave boy's warning. One moment, Brar and her cousin could hear his whistling echo through the night, and the next, it was gone, swallowed by an eerie silence. In its place came the unmistakable sound of a loud splash, like something heavy had fallen into the water."

Reet paused, as if the memory of the tale weighed heavily on her.

"A cold shiver ran down Brar's spine. She sat frozen, her breath quickening. Instinct told her to open the car window, but before she could act, her cousin shouted for her to stay inside and dashed toward the canal. She watched helplessly as he disappeared into the darkness, calling the mischievous boy's name. His voice grew more desperate, each shout unanswered. Then, without warning, the shouting stopped. The sudden silence that followed was more terrifying than any noise.

"Brar sat glued to her seat, her body rigid with fear, unable to move. It was as if every muscle in her body had betrayed her. She remained there, cold and trembling, paralyzed by the weight of uncertainty. Moments later, she heard a new sound as of something being dragged along the ground. The sound started faintly, growing louder as it drew closer to the car."

Reet leaned in slightly, her voice trembling with the tension of the narrative.

"The noise came from the front of the car, but her view was blocked by the raised bonnet. She knew she should check, but her body refused to obey. Fear gripped her so tightly that she could not even lift her head. She closed her eyes, hoping the sound would go away, but it grew louder, closer, inching past her window and heading toward the canal.

"Finally, when the dragging noise had faded into the distance, Brar's eyes drifted open against her better judgment. It was a decision she would regret for the rest of her life."

Reet's voice softened, as if trying to capture the terror Brar had felt.

"Brar looked toward the source of the sound, hoping to see her cousin safe and sound. And she did see him, but not as she had wished. He lay on the ground, unconscious, his face pressed into the mud. His arm was raised toward the sky, as though pointing to the moon, but it was not by his own will. Something invisible had clutched his arm and was dragging him toward the canal. Brar could see the soil shift beneath his limp body as it moved closer to the water's edge."

I could feel my breath catch as Reet's voice wavered.

"Brar fought to contain her fear, but it overwhelmed her. She let out a scream, sharp and full of panic. In an instant, the dragging stopped. Brar stared in horror as the air around her cousin seemed to ripple and shift. The invisible force dragging him began to take form. Slowly, the shape of a young girl materialized before Brar's eyes. The girl's features were pale, and her expression cold. The figure held Brar's cousin for a moment, then dissolved back into smoke, leaving him limp and lifeless on the ground."

     THE OTHER SIDE OF HORIZON

Reet paused briefly, her eyes distant, as if lost in the darkness of the tale.

"Brar could not process what she had just seen. Her body gave in to the terror, and everything went black. She fainted, collapsing inside the car, consumed by fear and disbelief.

"When she woke, she found herself in a hospital room, surrounded by her family and police officers. An old farmer had found her in the morning while passing by with his family. They had brought her to the hospital and notified the authorities. Brar lay in that bed, struggling to comprehend what had happened. Every time she tried to explain what she had seen, the officers dismissed it as the delusions of a traumatized mind. The doctors, convinced that she was suffering from shock, admitted her to a psychiatric ward for observation."

Reet's voice took on a somber tone as she continued.

"She stayed there for three days, trapped between doubt and fear. She began to question herself, wondering if what she had witnessed was real or just a figment of her imagination. Her father, desperate to help her, brought her home after those three days, but Brar was not the same. She started to lose her grip on reality, haunted by the events of that night."

Reet's gaze flickered toward the sky for a moment, before returning to me.

"On the third day after returning home, Brar's father brought three visitors to see her. They were from Arkha, a small village not far from where the incident had taken place. At first, Brar wanted nothing to do with them. She did not want to recount the story she had come to doubt herself. But the visitors insisted. Eventually, worn down by their persistence, she told them everything."

Reet's voice grew quieter, her words filled with a strange weight.

"To Brar's surprise, the visitors listened carefully, hanging onto every word as though they believed every detail. When she finished, the three men exchanged knowing glances, as if the pieces of a long-unsolved puzzle had finally come together.

"One of them, an older man with a deep, commanding voice, spoke. Brar later learned that he was the Sarpanch of Arkha, a leader in his village. His voice was steady, as if he were sharing an old, grim truth.

"'What you saw that night was not an illusion, my child,' he told her. 'For some time, we have suspected that these disappearances were the work of a restless spirit. There was a girl from our village, drowned in that same canal by her husband over a dowry dispute. A passerby tried to save her, but he was too late. She was already gone when he pulled her lifeless body from the water. Her husband fled and was never held accountable, and no case was ever filed against him.'

     THE OTHER SIDE OF HORIZON

"The old man paused for a moment, his expression heavy with sorrow.

"'The girl's spirit remains bound to that place, seeking revenge against men who wander near the canal at night. She uses the same method by which she was killed—drowning. She takes no pity on them, for in her eyes, they are no different from the man who took her life. But you survived because her vengeance is not aimed at women. She spared you, child, because you are not the enemy she seeks.'"

Reet finished the story with a solemn look on her face, as though the tale had taken something from her. The weight of the story lingered in the air between us, and for a moment, neither of us spoke.

The silence that followed was filled with the kind of understanding that only comes from hearing a truth too heavy to be ignored.

On hearing the old man's explanation, a strange feeling overtook Brar, an unsettling mixture of relief and sorrow. She was both allayed and distraught, unable to process the reality of what she had witnessed. Her emotions overwhelmed her, and it took many days for her to come to terms with the truth.

The villagers from Arkha, those same people who had visited her, soon established a small temple on the road where the murders had taken place. They prayed for the restless soul of the drowned girl, hoping to grant her the peace she never found in life. Strangely, after the temple was built, the mysterious deaths ceased entirely. The police, unaware of the spirit's presence, claimed credit for scaring off the supposed killer through their frequent patrols and drills.

Reet finished her story with a heavy sigh and stared into the night sky, her expression distant and solemn. A shiver ran down my spine, though I gave no outward sign of discomfort. I sat, stunned, unable to tear my mind away from the symmetry of the story. Every piece of the mystery fit together so flawlessly, and the supernatural element added a haunting chill that lingered.

"That was incredible, Reet," I said, my voice filled with genuine awe. "And that eerie, chilling touch was just brilliant. I love your story. It is mind-blowing. Honestly, you should consider becoming a writer someday; it suits you perfectly."

A painful smile flickered across her face, as though my compliment stirred both joy and sorrow within her. Breaking her long gaze at the sky, she stood and faced me, her expression shifting to something serious and somber.

"Stay in touch, Sam," she said quietly. "Now that I have found you after so many years, it would be hard for me if you went missing again."

I rose to my feet, smiling warmly at her words, and pulled her into a tight hug. "It won't happen again, my friend. Give me your number and email so we can stay in

     THE OTHER SIDE OF HORIZON

touch. And promise me you will try to visit me in Canada soon."

"I promise," she replied with a gentle smile, "if you promise to visit me here too."

She asked for my phone to save her contact. As she entered her number, a heaviness settled over me. Though I knew we would meet again, it was hard to walk away from the happiness I had found after so long. When she handed the phone back, she hugged me tightly one last time, and I held onto the moment, reluctant to let it slip away.

As she began walking away, she stopped once more, glancing over her shoulder. "Don't forget to call me when you get home."

I nodded and smiled, silently promising I would.

The next morning, I boarded my flight to Canada, carrying with me the warmth of our reunion. The disappointment I had felt over the failed project was drowned out by the joy of reconnecting with Reet. I could not stop thinking about the story she had told me. Her version of the events was so captivating that I even considered including it in my report as a creative addition. But in the end, I decided against it, knowing it would be more meaningful as a personal memory. If only I had been able to interview Brar herself, it would have been the perfect ending to the story.

The flight home took longer than expected, delayed by weather, but eventually, I arrived. After a long shower,

I lay down on my bed, smiling as I reflected on all the happy memories I had gathered during my time in India. I remembered my promise and decided to call Reet right away.

I grabbed my phone and scrolled through the contacts, searching for the number she had saved. When I found it, a strange feeling washed over me, an inexplicable sense of foreboding. Something struck me like a bolt of lightning, leaving me frozen in place. My mind raced, and my heart pounded as realization dawned.

I stared at the screen, my body rigid with disbelief. It was all there, clear as day. The name of one of the two boys involved in the final incident flashed vividly in my mind. I remembered his face,and his strong, athletic build as of a rugby player. I had met him before, a long time ago, back when Reet and I were still kids.

Everything started to make sense. The way Reet's story had tied up all the loose ends from my investigation, fitting the pieces together with uncanny precision. A chill ran through me as I comprehended the truth, the weight of it pressing down on me like a heavy shadow.

I stared down at my phone, the screen glowing ominously in the dim light. The contact saved under "Reet Singh Brar" confirmed everything.

Believe What You See

Let me begin my story with the first day of our trip when I took two days off to visit Raj's grandparents with him. We were close friends, like brothers, for the last fifteen years. Raj's grandparents lived in a farmhouse that had belonged to their family for over sixty years. They had a deep emotional connection to the place, so when Raj's parents moved to the city and invited them to join, they politely declined. They preferred to remain at the farmhouse, supervising its daily operations and continuing the life they had built.

The farmhouse was situated on a mountain slope, far from the noise of the city, on the outskirts of a quiet village called Kieran. A few days away from the constant rush of life sounded perfect to me. I had been planning this trip for months, eager to get away and enjoy some peace in the countryside with Raj.

At dawn, we reached the village that lay at the foot of the mountain. Raj pointed toward the farmhouse, and in the distance, we could see its lights flickering like tiny beacons through the misty morning air. As we made our way up the winding road in our vehicle, the farmhouse lights grew brighter, almost as if they were welcoming us. The chill in the air became sharper as we climbed higher, and we pulled our woollen clothes tighter around us, feeling like sheep huddling together for warmth.

There were two roads leading from the village to the farmhouse. One was a broad and smooth path, clearly meant for vehicles, while the other was steep, narrow, and rocky. It looked old, the kind of road that had once been used by horses and mules but was now overgrown and rarely travelled.

The excitement built as we drove higher. Raj had been praising the beauty of the place for months, and we could not wait to see it for ourselves. When we finally arrived, we stepped out of the vehicle and stood in awe. The farmhouse was enormous, perched perfectly on the slope of the mountain, offering a complete view of the little village nestled below. The lights in the village shimmered in different colors, like stars scattered across the land.

The farmhouse was surrounded by farmland, with an animal farm on one side and a small worker's cottage on the other. The only sound we could hear was the soft breeze moving through the trees. There was something special about the place, something that made even the sky appear more vivid. I had never seen so many stars before, and their brilliance felt surreal, as if we had stepped into a dream.

As we stood there, the front door of the farmhouse opened, and an elderly man stepped out. Though he was clearly in his seventies, his tall frame and strong physique were impressive enough to put most younger men to shame. He wore a thick leather jacket and a silk scarf draped elegantly around his neck, which gave him an air of quiet dignity. His neatly combed gray hair and closely trimmed beard hinted at the handsomeness he must have possessed in his younger days.

Raj's face lit up as he stepped forward to greet the man. "Dadaji," he called out with warmth, touching his grandfather's feet in a gesture of respect before embracing him tightly.

Raj's grandfather smiled, his expression gentle but lively, and hugged him back. Then, turning to us, he gave a welcoming smile and said, "Come in, boys. Make yourselves at home."

He called out for someone, and a younger man appeared, ready to show us to our rooms. Just as we were about to head inside, Raj darted a glance around the yard, his curiosity piqued.

"Where is Dadi?" he asked with a slight frown.

Raj's grandfather chuckled. "She has gone for her evening walk. The doctor has advised her to walk regularly to manage her diabetes. She did not want to go today, knowing you were arriving, but I insisted. She has been busy cooking for you all morning. Go ahead and get fresh in your rooms, and by the time you are ready, I will have the fire going in the living room for dinner."

We followed the man into the house, and as soon as we entered, we were struck by the grandeur of the place. The rooms were enormous, decorated with traditional furnishings that exuded an old-world charm. Everywhere we looked, we saw antiques and carefully preserved artifacts that gave the house a sense of history and class.

The room assigned to me was no less than a king's chamber. From the high ceilings to the richly upholstered furniture, everything felt luxurious and refined. The warmth of the room was inviting after the cold journey, and I wasted no time in filling the large bathtub with hot water. The bath was quick, but it left me feeling refreshed and ready for the evening ahead.

Hunger gnawed at me as I dressed, and I made my way downstairs with Raj and the others. As we descended the staircase, I could not help but admire the craftsmanship of the woodwork. The carvings on the railings were intricate and beautiful, and the paintings that adorned the walls were unlike anything I had seen before. The moonlight streaming in through the tall windows gave everything a soft, ethereal glow, adding to the charm of the house.

Raj led us to the living room, where his grandfather was already tending to the fireplace. The flames crackled and danced, casting a warm glow over the spacious room. Beside the fireplace stood an enormous bookshelf filled with old books, their spines weathered but dignified. A couple of leather couches were arranged near the fire, inviting us to sit and relax.

Across the room, a long dining table stood adorned with silverware that gleamed under the light of tall candles. The setting was elegant, almost regal, and we exchanged glances of amazement, impressed by the effort that had gone into making the evening special.

Just then, a door opened behind the dining table, and a woman stepped in. She was in her sixties, draped in a soft white shawl that gave her an air of grace and sophistication. Raj's face lit up with joy, and without hesitation, he rushed toward her.

"Dadi!" he exclaimed, his voice filled with affection.

His grandmother welcomed him with a warm smile and opened her arms. Raj greeted her with the same respect he had shown his grandfather, touching her feet and embracing her warmly.

"It has been so long, Dadi," Raj said, his eyes sparkling with affection. "You look younger every time I see you."

She laughed softly, her eyes twinkling with joy as she patted his cheek. Raj guided her toward us, introducing each of us in turn. She greeted us kindly, her voice soft but filled with warmth, and we immediately felt at ease in her presence.

After the introductions, we made our way to the dining table, where a feast awaited us. The food was nothing short of spectacular, every dish bursting with flavor and prepared with care. As we ate, the room filled with laughter and conversation. Raj's grandparents were unlike any elders we had ever met; open-minded, kind, and full of life. Their stories captivated us, and their hospitality made us feel completely at home.

The evening passed in a blur of good food, laughter, and warmth. It was clear to all of us why Raj held his grandparents in such high regard. There was a special charm about them, a quality that was rare and refreshing. We knew then that this trip would be one we would never forget.

After the dinner, we seated ourselves on the couch and proceeded with a game of cards. The wood in the chimney still burned bright, making the room feel warm and cozy as we sank into the comfortable leather couches. The crackling of the fire, mixed with the shuffle of cards, set a relaxed tone. We played a couple of rounds, enjoying the friendly competition, until fatigue crept in, and the game lost its excitement. Slowly, the conversation turned quieter, and we set the cards aside.

Raj's grandfather leaned back into his chair, his expression softening as he shared stories from his past. He spoke of his days in the military, his voice steady and filled with a sense of pride. The stories were captivating, filled with tales of camaraderie, adventure, and valuable lessons. Every word carried the weight of experience, drawing us deeper into his world. At one point, he brought out an old photo album containing black-and-white photographs from those days, showing us pictures of his younger self, standing tall in uniform with his comrades.

It was easy to see that Raj's grandfather had been a man of taste and discipline. The way he walked, spoke, and presented himself naturally commanded respect.

"I was not just a soldier," he said with a nostalgic smile. "I loved horses too. Horses are like old friends. They remember you, even when you have been away for a long time."

He stood and invited us to see a collection he had kept over the years. Opening a large cabinet, he revealed an impressive array of saddles, boots, caps, and whips. Each item looked meticulously maintained, a testament to his passion. We admired the craftsmanship and the obvious care he had taken to preserve them.

As we returned to our seats, my eyes fell on a particular whip displayed in a glass frame on a side table. It looked elegant, yet modest compared to the other whips we had just seen, which were laid openly on a rack. The handle had intricate carvings that caught the light from the fire, and there was something about it that seemed out of place.

Curious, I got up from my seat and walked over to examine it more closely. After a moment, I turned to Raj's grandfather and asked politely, "Does this whip hold some importance? What is so special about it that you have placed it in a frame, sir?"

Raj's grandfather exchanged a glance with his wife, who was sitting quietly at the far end of the room. He took a few pieces of wood and carefully placed them in the chimney, sending the flames dancing in the draught. I made my way back to my seat and settled in across from him, waiting for his response. His eyes met mine directly, and in his usual calm tone, he began to speak.

"Yes, it is dear to me because this is the first whip I ever owned. My father gave it to me when I was young. But that is not the only reason I placed it in a glass frame."

He paused, his gaze lingering on the whip.

"There is a story behind it. An incident that changed my view of the world."

I noticed a subtle shift in his expression that was something almost imperceptible, a flicker of emotion. Excited by this change and driven by my own curiosity, I leaned forward slightly and asked, "If you feel comfortable, would you mind telling us about it?"

He gave a small smile, his eyes twinkling with a hint of mischief. "Do you believe in ghosts?" he asked quietly.

The unexpected question left me momentarily stunned, and I glanced at Raj and the others. We exchanged bewildered looks, unsure of what to make of the question.

"No, sir," I replied politely. "I do not believe in ghosts."

He smiled again, the corners of his eyes crinkling. "Are you certain?"

"Yes, I am quite certain," I answered. "Ghost stories are just tales made up to scare children."

Raj's grandfather nodded thoughtfully. "Everyone is entitled to their beliefs," he said softly. Then he glanced out of the small window beside the chimney, his gaze distant as if recalling something from long ago. After a moment, he turned his head slowly toward his wife, who gave him an encouraging nod from across the room. He cleared his throat and leaned forward slightly, ready to begin.

"You asked me why the whip is in the frame, and I will tell you the story. I think you will find it strange, unlike anything you have ever heard before. It is a story that is difficult to believe, but it is the truth."

A wave of excitement surged through me. Even Raj, who had likely heard many of his grandfather's tales, looked intrigued. It was clear from his expression that this was not a story he had heard before. The way his grandfather spoke gave the impression that we were about to experience something unforgettable.

We settled deeper into our seats, waiting for him to begin. He sank into his chair, his voice calm and clear, every word measured and deliberate.

"It must have been nearly fifty years ago. I was still young, not more than twenty-five years old. I loved riding more than anything back then, and I was known as the best rider in the region. I even built the largest stable around these parts. But there was only one thing I loved more than riding," he said, casting a warm glance at his wife, "and she is sitting here with us tonight."

Raj's grandmother smiled, her eyes twinkling with affection, and gave him a playful nod of acknowledgment.

"It was the year Raj's father was born. He was just a few months old when he fell ill with a terrible fever. He cried endlessly, and nothing we did seemed to help. I brought the doctor from the village and insisted he stay with us overnight to care for the baby. It was a bitter winter night, and the only light in the room came from a lamp and a few flickering candles. The doctor examined the child thoroughly while I watched impatiently, desperate for a solution. After a long examination, the doctor turned to me and said that the only way to save him was to get medicine from the neighbouring village immediately."

Raj's grandfather paused, glancing into the fire as if seeing that cold winter night once more.

"It was late, and the wind outside was relentless. But time was against us, and I knew I had to go. We had no vehicles then, only horses, and I was the fastest rider around. I did not want to leave my wife and child, but I had no choice. I remember how Raj's grandmother instructed the attendants to prepare my horse. I rushed to my room to bundle up against the cold. Before leaving, I grabbed this very whip and mounted my horse. The journey ahead was not going to be easy."

The fire popped again, and the room seemed to grow quieter as we leaned in, drawn deeper into the story. Raj's grandfather continued, his voice steady and deliberate.

"The night was unforgiving, and the road to the village was treacherous. But I knew I had to push forward, no matter what awaited me on that path."

We waited breathlessly, sensing that the heart of the story was just beginning to unfold.

Descending the mountain was easy. The sky was clear, and with the light of the lamp flickering on my horse's side, the journey felt smooth and steady. I reached the village faster than I had imagined, but a significant amount of time was wasted searching for the right medicine.

The real challenge began when I started ascending the mountain. The wind had picked up, howling as it pushed against me. A half-moon peeked through the low-hanging clouds like a silver eye, casting pale beams on the path ahead. I urged the horse forward, but our pace slowed considerably, and no amount of effort could speed it up.

The cold was biting now, the wind cutting through my scarf like steel, making my face go numb. I pulled the scarf tighter, trying to escape the sting of the icy breeze, but it was relentless. We had been making slow but steady progress when, without any warning, the night was split by a loud, booming clap of thunder. There was no flash of lightning and just the deafening roar that shook the sky.

The horse reared slightly, startled by the sudden sound. It swerved off the narrow trail, and for a terrifying moment, I thought I would be thrown from the saddle. Fortunately, I had been riding at a slow pace, or things could have taken a far worse turn. Even so, the horse lost its footing on the rocky ground, slipping awkwardly and twisting its leg. A pained cry escaped from the animal, and it staggered before coming to a halt.

It was my best horse, the calmest and most reliable one in my stable. Had it been any other horse, I might have been thrown off and left injured on the mountainside. I slid off its back and carefully inspected the twisted leg. There was nothing I could do at the moment. I patted its neck reassuringly, freeing it from reins under a sturdy tree nearby.

"I will come back for you," I whispered, though the horse could only look at me with tired, pained eyes. There was no time to lose. I had to deliver the medicine and save my child.

With the lamp in one hand and the whip in the other, I began the climb up the mountain on foot. The wind had eased slightly but still gusted through the trees, rattling the leaves and sending a chill through the air. I pressed forward, determined to reach my home before it was too late.

As I hurried along the path, the night seemed to grow heavier around me. It was then that I heard it: A faint sound of footsteps shuffling behind me, as if someone was dragging their feet along the ground.

I stopped, raising the lamp to peer into the darkness behind me. The light illuminated only the narrow path and the dark outline of trees. There was no one in sight. I shook my head, telling myself it was nothing, just the sound of leaves or branches disturbed by the wind.

But as I started walking again, the footsteps resumed, matching my pace exactly. I stopped suddenly, and the steps behind me ceased as well. I turned around again, scanning the dark trail with my lamp held high, but there was only silence and shadows.

A nervous smile crept across my face. "It is just my imagination," I whispered, trying to steady my nerves.

I pressed forward, but no matter how far I walked, the footsteps stayed with me. They followed closely, as if something unseen was walking in my shadow. Every time I quickened my pace, the steps behind me did the same. When I slowed, they slowed too. It was as if I had gained an invisible companion on that lonely mountain path.

After a while, I stopped paying attention to the footsteps, forcing myself to focus on my destination. But then, the sound changed. The footsteps grew louder, faster and no longer the soft drag of someone walking lazily but the frantic pounding of someone running toward me. It sounded like a wild animal chasing down prey.

Terror surged through me. I spun around, gripping the whip tightly in my hand, ready to lash out at whatever was following me.

What I saw startled me to the core.

Standing a few feet away, illuminated by the pale light of the moon and the glow from my lamp, was a goat. Its eyes gleamed unnaturally, reflecting the light like two small orbs. Relief flooded over me at first seeing it was only a goat. I laughed at myself for being so spooked.

But as I turned to continue my journey, I heard the soft, deliberate footsteps again. They followed me relentlessly. I looked back, and there was the goat, trailing behind me without a sound, its shining eyes fixed on me.

Annoyed, I tried shooing it away several times. The goat would pause briefly when I yelled, only to resume following me a moment later. I grew frustrated and decided it was time to teach the animal a lesson.

With the whip raised, I turned to give it a firm lash, hoping to scare it off for good. But as the whip reached its apex, I froze. The goat was no longer there.

In its place stood a large, ferocious-looking dog, its eyes glowing with the same eerie light as the goat's had.

A chill ran down my spine. I backed away slowly, never taking my eyes off the creature. The dog did not move; it simply stood there, watching me with those strange, familiar gleaming eyes, as if waiting for something.

I swallowed hard and turned back toward the path, forcing myself to keep moving forward. The moon hung low in the sky, its silver light guiding my way, but the darkness seemed to press in closer with every step.

Just when I thought the nightmare could not grow worse, I heard the footsteps again. This time, they were soft, almost cautious, as if someone small and light was following me.

Dread crept into my chest as I turned once more, holding the lamp high.

A small figure stepped out of the shadows, illuminated by the moonlight. It was a boy, no older than seven or eight and his face pale and expressionless.

My heart stopped when I paid attention.

I didn't know which was more frightening, seeing a weird cold boy in the middle of nowhere, or knowing that he was the son of one of my farm workers whom I had buried a few days back..

He stared at me with lifeless eyes, the same glowing orbs I had seen in the goat and the dog. His head jerked slightly to the side, a movement so unnatural that it sent a violent shiver down my spine.

In that moment, I knew what had been haunting me all along.

Raj's grandfather paused, his face lit by the soft glow of the fire. His wide, unblinking eyes seemed to reflect the flames, giving him an otherworldly look. We sat frozen, captivated by the story, every muscle in our bodies tense with anticipation.

He leaned back, straightening his posture, and continued in a calm, measured voice.

"I had heard stories of this entity before and how it takes on the forms of animals, children, or even the dead to prey on the fear of those who cross its path. They call it Massan, an ancient being that feeds on terror and haunts the lonely places of the world. Some say it rests in water during the day and roams freely at night. Others believe it moves silently through the wilderness, drawn to those who are lost or vulnerable."

Raj's grandfather stared deeply into the fire, his voice steady but laden with the weight of the memory.

"That night, I realized the stories were true. Massan was no mere legend. It was real, and it had chosen me as its prey."

He paused, his gaze still locked on the flickering flames.

"I knew then that my only hope was to keep moving—to not let fear consume me, no matter how terrifying the path became."

The fire crackled softly, and the room remained silent as we waited for him to reveal how the encounter ended.

At that time I realized that the thing had been trying to scare me from the very start and was not something to be messed with. Suddenly, a shot of panic and terror took over me. It became hard to move, but then I thought of my baby. That thought gave me the strength to gather control over my frozen limbs. I turned back and started heading in the direction of the house. Though I knew the farmhouse was not far, I also realized that the remaining few yards would be the hardest part of the journey.

I forced myself to keep moving, ignoring the sound of footsteps behind me. Every muscle in my body was tense, but I focused on placing one foot in front of the other. To keep my calm, I began humming a song, the tune shaky at first but slowly gaining rhythm as I pressed forward.

The footsteps grew louder, gaining on me with every step, as if whoever or whatever was behind me was not ready to let me go. The flame in the lamp flickered wildly in the wind, casting strange, dancing shadows across the dark trail. I tightened my grip on the lamp and whip, knowing I had to keep moving no matter what.

As I walked, the nature of the footsteps shifted erratically, changing from calm to violent and then back again, as though whatever was following me was taunting me, playing with me. And then I heard it, a second set of footsteps, coming from my side. I did not want to look, but curiosity got the better of me, and I glanced from the corner of my eye.

There, walking beside me, was a small dog, its fur shimmering faintly under the dim moonlight. I tried to keep my eyes on the road ahead, forcing myself to ignore it, but the footsteps kept changing. Whenever I dared to glance again, the dog was no longer a dog and it became a larger animal, then a cat, and then, to my horror, a woman walking silently beside me.

Every time I looked, the figure beside me changed, shifting into something new, something more unsettling. I picked up my pace, hoping to outrun the apparitions, but they kept matching me step for step, drawing closer with every passing second. My breath grew heavy, and my heart pounded in my chest.

Just when I thought I could not take it any longer, I saw a glimmer of hope ahead. A faint light flickered in the distance and the warm glow of the farmhouse, promising safety. The sight gave me renewed strength, and I resolved to make a run for it.

But as I prepared to dash toward the light, the thing walking beside me morphed again. This time, it took the form of a ball, bouncing playfully in front of me, as if daring me to play along. I froze, my heart hammering in my chest. Though I knew it was just a ball, fear held me in place, paralyzing my limbs.

For a few agonizing moments, I stood there, torn between fear and the urgent need to reach the house. I knew I could not afford to waste any more time. My son needed the medicine. I clenched the whip tighter, reminding myself of what was at stake.

With all the strength my exhausted body could muster, I lashed out at the ball with the whip. The crack echoed sharply through the night as the ball bounced away, disappearing into the dark terrain to my left.

As soon as the ball vanished, a piercing sound filled the air and the unmistakable cry of a baby, coming from the very spot where the ball had disappeared.

Every instinct told me not to look back. I fixed my gaze on the farmhouse and ran as fast as my legs would carry me. The sound of the crying baby faded behind me, swallowed by the night, and I did not stop until I reached the warm glow of the house.

Standing in the circle of light cast by the farmhouse, I felt an overwhelming sense of relief. The light was like a shield, wrapping me in warmth and safety. It felt as though I had crossed some invisible boundary, leaving the nightmare behind me.

I handed the medicine to the doctor without saying a word about what had happened on the trail. He administered it to my son, and within a couple of days, the fever broke. My son began to recover, and the threat that had loomed so large over our family started to fade.

But my own ordeal was far from over.

Not long after delivering the medicine, I fell gravely ill. A fever unlike any I had ever known took hold of me, burning through my body like the desert sun. I was paralyzed, unable to move or speak, my body refusing to obey my will.

Raj's grandmother called every doctor she could find, but none of them could bring the fever down. Day after day, I lay in that bed, helpless, as the fever raged on. It seemed like there was no end in sight. Every healer who saw me shook their heads in despair, convinced that there was no cure.

For an entire month, exactly thirteen days, the fever held me in its grip. I hovered between life and death, unsure if I would ever recover. And then, just as suddenly as it had come, the fever released me. One morning, I woke up feeling lighter, as if a great burden had been lifted from my soul. Within days, I was back on my feet, riding my horse as if nothing had happened.

When the villagers heard of my recovery, they came to visit, bringing with them their stories and superstitions. They all said the same thing and the fever had been a punishment. They believed that my encounter with the Massan, and the act of striking at it with the whip, had angered the spirit.

According to their beliefs, the Massan is not a being that can be fought or challenged. It thrives on fear, but it

    THE OTHER SIDE OF HORIZON

does not tolerate defiance. My act of defiance had made it furious, and the fever had been its way of exacting retribution.

Some of the elders urged me to destroy the whip, saying that it had been cursed by coming into contact with the spirit. But I could not bring myself to part with it. This whip was more than just a tool and it was a gift from my father, the only thing I had left to remember him by after the war claimed both him and my mother.

So, instead of destroying it, I placed it in this glass frame, where it has remained ever since. No one has touched it, and no one ever will."

Raj's grandfather leaned back in his chair, the firelight casting flickering shadows across his face.

The room fell silent, the weight of the story settling over us like a thick blanket. I glanced around and saw that everyone was lost in thought, their faces pale and tense. The tale had left us all speechless, each of us trying to process what we had just heard.

I felt a strange mix of awe and unease, not knowing whether to dismiss the story as an elaborate fiction or accept it as something far more unsettling. But one thing was certain, the way Raj's grandfather told it, with that calm, unwavering voice, made it feel all too real.

I shifted in my seat, breaking the silence with an awkward laugh. "Well, that was... quite the story," I said, trying to lighten the mood.

But no one joined in my laughter. They all sat still, their faces etched with something that looked a lot like fear.

"Twenty-seven years, I have lived and have never seen any ghost as yet, and this Massan sure sounds like a stupid guy," I said, trying to hold back my laughter.

It caught Raj off guard. He gave me a sharp look, one that instantly made me feel foolish for being so dismissive. I could tell he was not pleased with my flippant remark. Regret washed over me as I realized I had sounded like an arrogant fool. Thankfully, Raj's grandfather stepped in to defuse the awkward tension.

"As I said before, son," his grandfather began with a calm, measured tone, "it is your choice and yours alone. I would not have believed in it either if it were not for what happened that night. You have every right to doubt. In life, you should believe in what you see, not just in what others tell you." His voice remained steady, but it carried the weight of experience, as he sat in his grand chair with the composure of a king. The firelight reflected in his eyes, which still burned with an inner glow that spoke of stories untold.

Raj's grandmother stood gracefully and smiled warmly. "Goodnight, boys," she said gently, her voice filled with affection as she took her leave. We all rose to bid her goodnight, and after the awkward pause that followed my careless words, we decided it was time to end the evening.

The rest of our stay at the farmhouse was nothing short of magical. Raj's grandparents treated us with unmatched warmth and hospitality, making us feel like honored guests. Their love and care enveloped us like a blanket, making every moment spent with them feel special. Before we knew it, the days flew by, and we were back to our busy lives, immersed in the routines of work and responsibility. Yet the memories of the farmhouse lingered in our minds, like echoes of a dream we did not want to let go.

A few days passed, and I found myself struggling to adjust to the demands of city life once again. The peace I had experienced at the farmhouse felt distant, like a fleeting moment I could not reclaim. One evening, on a rare day off, I received an urgent call from my workplace.

There had been a critical system failure at the factory, and the situation required immediate attention. The call came from the highest-ranking manager, leaving me no choice but to get there as quickly as possible. I arrived at the factory and worked alongside my team, laboring tirelessly for hours. By the time the issue was finally resolved, it was well past two in the morning. Exhausted but relieved, I was pleased to hear that the manager had granted me the following day off as a small compensation for my effort.

I borrowed a friend's bike since my car was still at the service station. Riding a bike was never my preference, but on that night, it felt strangely fitting. The cool night breeze brushed against my skin, the clouds above scattered in dark patches, and the empty road stretched ahead, inviting me into the peaceful silence of the early morning.

As I cruised along the deserted road, the sky suddenly opened up, unleashing a torrential downpour. The rain was unforgiving, pouring in thick streams that drenched me within moments. It was no ordinary rain; it felt as if nature had decided to test my endurance. Left with no other choice, I sought refuge at a small bus stop along the roadside.

The shed was modest, offering little more than a few chairs and a flickering light bulb overhead. But it was enough to shield me from the relentless downpour. As I shook off the water from my clothes, I noticed I was not alone. In the far corner of the shed stood a man, extraordinarily tall, with a posture so still that he could have been mistaken for a statue.

At first, I paid him little attention, too preoccupied with the cold that seeped through my wet clothes. I rubbed my hands together in a futile attempt to generate warmth and stop my shivering. I glanced at my wristwatch, only to realize that it had stopped working. Frustrated, I took out my mobile phone to check the time and was relieved to find it still functioning.

"It sure came down hard," I said aloud, hoping to spark a conversation with the stranger. "Impossible to ride in this rain."

The man did not respond. He stood in the corner like a shadow, unmoving and silent. His silence felt unsettling, but I shrugged it off. I scanned the surroundings and saw no vehicle nearby, which made me wonder if he was waiting for a bus or for someone to pick him up.

Curiosity got the better of me, and I tried again. "I work for Basant Logistics, not far from here. Do you work in one of the factories nearby?" I asked, hoping for some interaction.

Once again, there was no reply. The man remained as still as a rock, as though he had not even registered my presence. His indifference began to annoy me. I told myself it was not worth the effort and decided to leave as soon as the rain let up.

When the rain finally slowed to a drizzle, I headed toward the bike without saying another word to the man. I kick-started the engine and, as I turned my head to look back at him, I noticed something strange. The man was not as tall as I had initially thought. He stood around six feet, give or take an inch. Puzzled but unwilling to dwell on it, I focused on getting home.

As I rode through the drizzle, the cold wind stung my face, and the raindrops, though smaller now, felt like tiny stones hitting my skin. I hummed a tune to myself, trying to shake off the lingering unease.

It was not long before I passed a man walking along the roadside. Something about him felt eerily familiar.

He wore the same clothes as the silent man from the bus stop. A chill ran down my spine as I sped up, hoping to put distance between us.

A few minutes later, I saw him again, standing by the roadside. This time, he was taller, close to seven feet. My heart raced as the eerie sense of recognition grew stronger.

I pushed the bike to its limits, but it did not matter. No matter how fast I went, I kept seeing him again and again, each time looking slightly different; first taller, then shorter, then even taller than before.

The fear gnawed at me, making it hard to concentrate. My hands trembled on the handlebars, and the bike wobbled dangerously. The memory of Raj's grandfather's story about Massan resurfaced in my mind, and with it came the dreadful realization that my mockery had not gone unnoticed.

I glanced to the side and saw him walking calmly beside me, as if my speed meant nothing to him. No matter how hard I accelerated, he remained there, his presence as steady as a shadow.

Panic seized me, clouding my thoughts. I knew I was in trouble, that I had invited this terror upon myself with my foolish arrogance. Just when I thought I would lose control entirely, I spotted a glimmer of hope ahead—a pair of headlights from an oncoming vehicle.

The sight of the approaching light was like a lifeline. I sped toward it, my heart pounding in my chest. As I

     THE OTHER SIDE OF HORIZON

neared the vehicle, the man vanished as suddenly as he had appeared, leaving nothing but the night behind him.

Relief washed over me, but it was short-lived. The wet road betrayed me, and the bike skidded violently. The world spun around me, and I hit the ground hard, losing consciousness.

When I opened my eyes, daylight greeted me. Pain radiated from every part of my body, and I found myself wrapped in bandages. Raj stood by my bedside, his face a mixture of relief and concern.

"You gave us a scare," he said with a small smile. "What happened?"

For a moment, I struggled to recall the events of the night. But as the memories came rushing back, so did the fear.

"Do you want to talk about it?" Raj asked, sensing my hesitation.

I met his gaze and nodded slowly. "Yes. I believe your grandfather now. Massan is real... and I have seen it."

The room fell silent as Raj processed my words. There was no longer any doubt—some stories are not just stories.

The Lady in the Potrait

"THE SUPERNATURAL IS THE NATURAL NOT YET UNDERSTOOD"

I believe, in everyone's life, comes a point, when he has to make a decision; a decision to stand by all the beliefs he has lived by most of his life, the very same beliefs which he has just seen shattered into pieces right before his eyes or he can make a decision to blow away the shattered pieces with a single breath of dismay and stray into the path of this new disclosure.

I had worked very hard in my profession of IT and sacrificed many things along my way to success in the industry. I sacrificed many friends, my hobbies, and even my family. I always wanted to be successful, and money was my main objective, and now when I had them both, I realized the importance of being loved unconditionally.

After three years in which I had seldom contacted my family, it was all of a sudden that I decided to pay my family a surprise visit because of this unexplainable urge.

And thus it happened one cloudy evening; I stood before my house in Mumbai and rang the bell. Far inside, I could hear the faint footsteps of someone stepping down the stairs, and somehow I could tell that the footsteps were of my mother. A moment later, the shabby door opened, revealing a woman standing by it.

Mother, dressed as I have always remembered her in a neatly tied white sari, smiled at me with an innocent honeyed smile on her oval pale face and watery eyes. She looked old, tired, and her face even paler than I remembered. With those same watery eyes, she embraced me warmly and tightly, as if never wanting to let go.

Just then, the door next to me opened, and a girl in her early twenties appeared. It took me a few moments to realize that it was my sister, Veerta. I could sense the happiness she felt upon seeing me, but she kept her emotions concealed behind an air of formality. She stepped forward and shook hands with me—a flabby, disinterested sort of handshake and turned to our mother, saying,

"Mother, I will put the luggage in his room."

She left, dragging my stroller behind her.

Veerta and I had always had a complicated relationship, filled with disagreements since childhood. Although she was only five years younger than me, we never truly understood each other. During her teenage years, as I entered adulthood, the distance between us grew. She was stubborn and rigid, much like me, and every argument felt as if I were arguing with a reflection of myself.

When I chose to pursue my career, disappearing from family life, Veerta took it personally. She was not impressed by my decision to stay away for so long, and the rare phone calls I made seemed to drive the wedge even deeper. Eventually, she refused to speak to me altogether. I knew that it was partly my fault because I never made a sincere effort to bridge the gap. Now, standing in our old house, a part of me wanted to change all that, to start fresh. Yet I had no idea where or how to begin.

Mom informed me that Dad was out of town for work and would not return for another five days. She wanted to surprise him with my visit, so she decided to keep it a secret. I made my way upstairs to my old room, where everything seemed frozen in time, just as I had left it years ago.

The sight of the familiar space stirred something inside me. Nostalgia washed over me like a wave, bringing with it memories of late nights spent studying, moments of joy, and the comfort of knowing that no matter what happened, this room had always been mine. With those thoughts swirling in my mind, I decided to take a hot shower, hoping it would clear my head and ease the emotional weight I felt pressing on my chest.

I arrived at the dining table to find mom and my sister arguing over something. Veerta was pleading for some

     THE OTHER SIDE OF HORIZON

permission, and mom shook her head in denial. I stood and listened to the argument for a while, and from what I heard, it was clear that Veerta had plans to go on a shooting project to some place in Darjeeling with her friends before they backed out at the crucial moment. Now, she wanted to go alone on the project, and it appeared to be of great importance to her, as I heard her call it a career-defining opportunity.

Mom, however, would not allow her to go alone. Veerta was a photographer by profession, and for as long as I could remember, she had been crazily driven by the love for nature and capturing it on camera.

I decided to step in, and the discussion ended abruptly with my appearance. I placed myself on the chair near mom, opposite my sister, and started filling my plate with the delicious food on the table. I began eating while mom and I did most of the talking. The only time Veerta spoke was when she passed me a bowl of mixed vegetables, reminding me how I used to love the dish. It was the first time she had talked directly to me on this trip.

We finished dinner, and while my sister helped mom clear the table, an urge to make a new start welled up inside me, and I decided to speak.

"Why won't you let her go, mom? It is important to her," I said in a polite voice.

Somehow, my words took both of them by surprise, catching them off guard. I had never interfered in my sister's life, so their reaction was understandable. Veerta was more surprised than mom to hear my words. Mom took a moment to recover from the surprise before she spoke with a tone of utter dominance.

"How can I, Avi? I cannot send her alone so far from home. It was hard enough for me to let her go with her friends, but I agreed because of the importance of the project. I cannot go with her to a remote village in Darjeeling because of my health, and there is no way I will send her alone."

I shifted my gaze toward Veerta, who looked dejected by the decision.

"How long is your trip, and when are you planning to leave?" I asked her.

"Four days, and I was supposed to leave the day after tomorrow," she answered in a sad and low voice.

I turned my head toward mom, who was now busy clearing the table, and spoke again in the same monotone as before.

"Let her go, mom. I will go with her."

I knew my words were about to draw too much attention, so I found it wise to retreat to my room. I caught a glimpse of the astonished looks on their faces from the corner of my eye and, in a hurry, bid them both goodnight and left.

　　THE OTHER SIDE OF HORIZON

I slept like a child that night, perhaps due to the fatigue from the trip. I woke up the next morning to the sound of a voice and the feeling of someone shaking me gently. I opened my eyes to find Veerta sitting beside me, her hand on my shoulder, wearing a worried expression.

"Are you alright, Avi? Mom sent me to wake you up. It is already lunchtime, and you are still sleeping."

"Yes, I am fine. I was just tired from all the travel and everything. You can tell mom that I will be downstairs in ten minutes," I replied while yawning and trying hard not to fall asleep again.

I closed my eyes one last time, then forced myself to get up. Veerta was at the door, about to leave, when she suddenly stopped at the entrance with her back to me.

"Thanks for coming with me on the trip. It is really important to me, and it is good to see you home after such a long time," she said in a quiet tone and then left immediately.

Her words lingered in the room, leaving me to sit for a moment, processing everything. It felt strange to hear her speak that way in such a genuine, almost vulnerable fashion. I realized this trip meant more than just a photography project to her. It was her way of reaching out, trying to rebuild the bridge that had fallen between us over the years. And perhaps, it was a chance for me to do the same.

I got up, dressed quickly, and went downstairs to find mom setting the table for lunch. The smell of freshly made chapatis and lentils filled the air. Veerta was already at the table, quietly helping mom arrange everything.

"Come, Avi. Lunch is ready," mom called warmly as I approached the table.

The three of us sat together, and for the first time in years, it felt like a real family moment. Mom and I carried most of the conversation, but Veerta chimed in now and then, her words brief but enough to show that the ice between us was beginning to thaw.

After lunch, mom pulled me aside while Veerta went back to her room.

"Avi, thank you for offering to go with her. It means a lot. You know she never says it, but she missed you."

I nodded, feeling a warmth spread through me that I had not felt in years.

The next two days passed quickly. Veerta was busy packing her photography equipment while I made sure everything was in order for the trip. It felt strange, yet good, to be doing this together. The tension between us was still there, but it was lighter now, like a burden that was slowly being lifted.

The morning of our departure arrived, and mom stood by the door, watching us with a mix of worry and pride as we loaded our bags into the taxi.

"Take care of each other," she said as we prepared to leave. "And call me when you reach."

"We will, mom," I assured her with a smile.

Veerta gave her a quick hug, then climbed into the back seat of the taxi. I followed her, and soon we were on our way to the station. The ride was quiet, with only the sound of the radio playing softly in the background. Veerta looked out the window, lost in thought, while I stole glances at her, trying to imagine what she was thinking.

At the station, we boarded the train bound for New Jalpaiguri. As the train pulled away from the platform, the city slowly gave way to open fields, forests, and distant hills.

Veerta spent most of the journey with her camera in hand, capturing every fleeting moment from the passing landscapes to the life inside the train. Watching her through the lens, I saw something I had not noticed before. Photography was not just her passion; it was her way of connecting with the world, a way to express what words could not.

We spoke intermittently during the journey, mostly light conversations, but they felt different this time as they were more honest, more meaningful. It was as if we were slowly rediscovering who we were to each other.

As the sun began to set, casting a warm orange glow over the fields, Veerta lowered her camera for a moment and looked out at the horizon.

"Thanks, Avi," she said softly, not turning to face me. "For coming along."

I smiled, feeling that this trip was about more than just a photography project. It was about us finding our way back to each other, one small step at a time.

The rhythmic clatter of the train wheels lulled us into a comfortable silence. By the time we reached New Jalpaiguri, the first light of dawn was breaking over the horizon. From there, we hired a taxi to take us up the winding roads to Darjeeling, the cool mountain air filling our lungs as the mist-covered hills welcomed us.

We were in Darjeeling's station the next day, and from there, we took a cab to reach a small village on the outskirts, nestled to the west of the Lesser Himalayas. Upon our arrival, we were greeted by officials from the company that had hired Veerta for the project. They introduced us to our guide, a local man named Sawant, who was assigned to escort us to the cottage where the supplies for our stay had already been stocked.

The cottage, once used by forest guards, had long been abandoned but was allocated to us for Veerta's work. It was located three miles west of the camp, isolated deep in the forest, and Veerta was assigned the task of shooting the western part of the forest for her project.

The path leading to the cottage was narrow and winding, with tall fir trees looming above us. The wind howled through the branches, as if warning us of an impending storm. The sky, now heavily overcast, sent shivers through us, and the scent of damp earth filled the air.

Sawant kept glancing up at the sky as we walked. "A storm is coming," he muttered more than once, his tone laced with certainty.

He made light conversation, explaining the forest's layout and pointing out locations where Veerta could capture stunning shots. He seemed knowledgeable and friendly, though his unease about the weather was hard to miss.

We finally arrived at the cottage, which stood at the center of a large clearing, as if nature had reluctantly allowed the building to exist within its domain. The garden surrounding it was wild and overgrown, as though the forest was reclaiming its territory. The structure itself, though old, was still well-maintained, with sturdy walls and a wooden porch that creaked underfoot as we stepped onto it.

Sawant switched on the porch light, and the glow brought a warm, welcoming aura to the otherwise eerie surroundings. He walked us through the layout of the cottage. It was a simple structure, built in a traditional style, with two bedrooms, a small living room, and a newly constructed bathroom attached to one corner.

The cottage had three points of entry: the main door that opened onto the porch, a smaller kitchen door that also connected to the porch, and a third, older door leading from the storeroom to the backyard. The wooden fences surrounding the property were worn but still stood tall, encircling the clearing like a protective boundary.

Inside, the kitchen was stocked with all the provisions we would need for the next few days. Sawant pointed out the generator in the storeroom, which would power the cottage's inverter, as there was no external source of electricity. He explained that the generator would need to be run regularly to keep the batteries charged.

By the time we finished inspecting the cottage, the rain had started to fall, light at first, then steadily increasing. The sound of raindrops drumming on the roof filled the air, creating an oddly soothing rhythm.

Just as we finished the tour, the sky unleashed a light drizzle. The soft patter of raindrops on the leaves echoed through the forest, hinting at the storm's approach.

Sawant gathered his belongings, ready to leave before the storm intensified. Just as he reached the gate, he hesitated. Something seemed to trouble him, and he hurried back up the porch steps toward us.

However, just as he reached the main gate, he stopped abruptly. A strange look passed across his face, and he turned back toward us, hurrying up the porch steps. His expression was tense, and his voice, when he spoke, carried a warning laced with concern.

"Sir, you and madam are kind people, so I cannot leave without giving you some advice." He glanced toward the forest as if expecting something to emerge from its shadows.

Curious, I nodded for him to continue.

"You may come across old houses deep in these woods," he began, his voice low and cautious. "They were once homes of villagers but were abandoned many years ago. If you stumble upon any such place, stay away. Those houses have been claimed by darkness. Evil lingers there, waiting for curious souls to stray too close."

I was taken aback by the gravity of his words. It felt like a line from a movie, and for a moment, I struggled to suppress the laughter bubbling inside me. I could see Veerta standing by the door, biting her lip to hold back a giggle.

Still, I managed to respond respectfully, "Thank you for the warning, Sawant. We will be careful."

Sawant gave a slight bow, satisfied with my answer, and disappeared into the forest path, the drizzle now turning into steady rain.

Veerta finally let out a soft laugh as the door closed behind us. "That was... something," she said, amusement dancing in her eyes.

I chuckled too. "Yeah, dark houses filled with evil spirits? Sounds like we just walked into a horror movie."

"Let's hope it stays just a story," Veerta said playfully, though a flicker of curiosity lingered in her tone.

"Thank you. I will keep that in mind. Hope to see you after three days."

Sawant gave a nod of approval and walked away, disappearing down the forest path.

With a small smile on my face, I strolled past Veerta's room. She was busy unpacking her bags, humming softly to herself. We spent the rest of the evening exploring the cottage, setting our belongings in place, and enjoying the peaceful atmosphere. Dinner was simple, and the sound of light rain tapping on the roof provided a soothing backdrop. Exhausted from the journey, we decided to retire to our rooms early.

The night stretched long and cold. As we lit a few lanterns to brighten the dim rooms, I hoped the storm would pass soon, leaving us with clear skies for Veerta's project. Little did I know that the storm outside would be nothing compared to the strange events that lay ahead.

The steady drizzle continued through the night, lulling me into a deep sleep. When I woke the next morning, the smell of coffee drifted through the air. I made my way to the porch, where I found Veerta seated with her laptop, a steaming mug of coffee beside her. She looked relaxed, her fingers tapping away at the keys as the morning mist hovered over the forest.

"I made some coffee and sandwiches for you," she said without looking up.

Her gesture brought a faint smile to my face. I appreciated not having to make breakfast myself. "Thanks," I replied, heading into the kitchen to grab my share.

I returned to the porch and sat beside her, taking in the serene morning as I sipped my coffee. Veerta had closed her laptop by now and was busy prepping her camera, carefully inspecting the lenses and equipment she would need for the day.

The tall fir trees stood silent, towering over the landscape like ancient guardians, while dark clouds slowly gathered above them, readying themselves for an imminent storm. I glanced at the sky and remembered Sawant's words.

"A storm is coming," I said, mimicking his tone, which made Veerta laugh softly.

She seemed genuinely happy and at ease, fully immersed in her work and the adventure ahead. We spent a few minutes reminiscing about our childhood, chatting about old memories. It felt good to reconnect, to bridge the gap that had grown between us over the years.

Soon, we gathered our things and left the cottage, following the path up the mountains. The directions Sawant had given us were precise, leading us to a breathtaking viewpoint. Veerta eagerly began capturing the landscape on camera, her eyes gleaming with excitement. I stood beside her, utterly mesmerized by the vast expanse of nature unfolding before us—rolling hills, thick forests, and mist-laden valleys. I hadn't realized how captivating the wilderness could be.

The peaceful moment, however, did not last long. The wind picked up strength, swirling through the forest with a fierce howl. Dark clouds moved rapidly across the sky, and distant flashes of lightning cut through the horizon. Moments later, a deafening crack of thunder echoed across the hills, shaking the forest to its core.

The once-majestic trees, standing tall and unwavering, now bowed to the relentless fury of the wind. Branches groaned and swayed, their leaves scattering like confetti caught in a storm.

Then, the rain began. Light at first, but it quickly escalated into a torrential downpour. Water poured from the sky in sheets, as if the heavens had unleashed all their might. Our raincoats and umbrella were no match for the deluge. The icy rain soaked us to the bone, and with the temperature dropping rapidly, it became unbearable to stay outside.

"We need to find shelter," I shouted over the roaring wind, barely able to hear my own voice.

Veerta nodded in agreement, shivering from the cold as we stumbled through the forest. We could hardly see where we were going, the rain blinding our path.

After what felt like an eternity, we spotted an old, abandoned house nestled among the overgrowth, about two kilometers from the cottage. It was a desolate place with vines coiled around the walls, and weeds had taken over what must once have been a beautiful garden. The windows were broken, and the wooden porch sagged under the weight of neglect.

We rushed to the porch, grateful for the refuge from the punishing rain. As we stood there, catching our breath, the chill of the wind seeped through our wet clothes. The shelter offered some relief, but the cold air bit at our skin, making it difficult to stay warm.

I looked at Veerta, whose teeth were chattering despite her efforts to hide it. "We can't stay here for long. This place won't keep us warm."

She nodded, hugging herself tightly to preserve what little warmth she had left. The house felt eerie, abandoned for years, as if the forest had reclaimed it. I glanced through the broken windows, trying to peer into the dark interior, but the shadows inside seemed thick, as if hiding secrets best left undisturbed. We had no choice but to stop here. The storm showed no signs of abating, and there was no way we could make it back to the cottage in these conditions.

"We'll wait until the rain slows down, then make our way back," I said.

Veerta nodded, her hands rubbing her arms for warmth. The wind howled around us, rattling the loose boards of the porch, as if the storm was determined to keep us there longer.

The forest loomed silently beyond the garden, the towering trees swaying in unison as the storm raged on. We waited in silence, listening to the rain drum against the roof and the occasional groan of the wind. Time seemed to stretch, the storm showing no mercy.

A faint smile broke out on Veerta's freezing face as she turned towards me and mimicked the voice of our escort from the other day.

"The abandoned houses have been claimed by the darkness and evil dwells in such places. Beware, Trespassers."

Her words brought a smile to my face despite the biting cold. I glanced at the old, weathered door and, with mock politeness, said, "Excuse me, but may we come in and take shelter?"

As if in response, a fierce gust of wind howled through the forest, and the main door made a long, screeching sound as it swayed on rusty hinges. The lock appeared broken, probably for years, leaving the door slightly ajar. We exchanged a quick glance, and without hesitation, decided to step inside. Staying outside was no longer an option with the cold wind cutting through us like knives.

The inside of the house was no more welcoming than the storm. The air was heavy with dust, and most of the window panes were shattered. An old table with three chairs stood at the center, the only furniture left behind, while the walls stood bare, except for one side where an old picture hung in a frame.

We slipped out of our wet raincoats, tossing them in a corner, and Veerta sat cross-legged on the dusty floor, inspecting her gear to make sure nothing was damaged by the rain. I was drawn to the picture on the wall. The glass of the frame was so murky that I had to pull a tissue from my pocket to wipe away the grime.

As I cleaned the surface, the image beneath it became clearer. It was an old fading photograph of a man and a woman standing in what looked like this very house. The woman wore a traditional red bridal dress, her beauty captured in a simple, timeless manner. There was a captivating charm in her gaze, a gentle serenity that seemed to hold my attention longer than I had expected. The man, dressed in traditional village attire, stood beside her with a modest expression, a stark contrast to the bride's vibrant presence.

I stared at the photograph for a few moments, lost in thought, before showing it to Veerta. She glanced at it with mild interest but quickly returned to her camera, unenthused by the old photo.

We took seats on the creaky chairs, the wood groaning under our weight, and Veerta began showing me the pictures she had taken earlier. The way she captured the forest's beauty, even through the veil of rain, was breathtaking. It was in these moments I realized just how talented she was with her eye for detail, her instinct to catch fleeting moments most people would overlook.

We talked for a while, letting nostalgia carry us back to our childhood. We laughed about old memories, teasing each other, and for a brief moment, the cold and eerie atmosphere of the house faded into the background. It felt good to reconnect with her in this way, breaking the barriers that had grown between us over the years.

The storm outside slowly began to calm, and the pounding rain diminished to a light drizzle. However, the wind persisted, snaking through the cracks in the walls and windows, its howling sound echoing through the empty rooms. Despite the relative calm, the cold air crept over us, sending chills down our spines.

Veerta rubbed her hands together, trying to fight off the cold, and I exhaled deeply, watching my breath form small clouds in the icy air.

"Do you think we should stay a little longer, or head back to the cottage?" she asked, her voice low and uncertain.

"Let's give it a few more minutes," I replied.

Finally, the storm gave up, and our journey back to the cottage was exhausting, with the path now slippery from the relentless rain. We reached the cottage well before nightfall, but the trek had taken its toll. Hungry and worn out, we raided the kitchen for some sausages and kebabs, which gave us the energy we badly needed.

After our meal, we settled into the living room. I lost myself in a book while Veerta reviewed her work from the day on her laptop, occasionally smiling at some of the shots she had taken. The day had drained us, and sooner than usual, we decided to call it a night. I went to my room, slipped under the covers, and fell asleep almost instantly.

But the night didn't offer peace. My sleep was restless, interrupted by strange feelings that I couldn't place. I would wake up intermittently, gasping for air as if suffocating, only to sit up in confusion. The unease in the room was thick, pressing against me like a heavy, invisible force. I reached for the water on my bedside table and took a few sips, trying to shake off the discomfort.

Slipping back into sleep, I found myself lost in the strangest, most unsettling dreams—shadows shifting, faces I couldn't recognize, and whispers too faint to comprehend. My mind seemed to drift further into the surreal, when suddenly, a loud scream jolted me awake.

It had come from Veerta's room.

In an instant, I switched on the bedside lamp, jumped out of bed, and rushed to her room, heart pounding in my chest. I flung her door open and hurriedly switched on the light, flooding the room with brightness.

There she was, sitting upright on her bed, wide-eyed and drenched in sweat.

I sprinted to her side as she scrambled off the bed and clung to me tightly, her whole body trembling. I could feel her rapid, shallow breaths against my chest. Her arms locked around me with desperate force, and I held her close, trying to steady her shaking frame.

Her heart was pounding so violently that I could feel it through her ribcage. I reached over and switched on the small bedside lamp, casting a softer, warmer glow in the room.

"Everything is fine, Veer. I am here with you," I whispered, keeping my voice low and soothing. "What happened?"

She didn't reply, her breath still ragged as she buried her face against my shoulder. I had never seen her like this as she was always been the brave one. Even when she was scared, she would try to act tougher, especially with me around. But this time was different. Something had truly rattled her.

I gently stroked her hair, patting her head in an attempt to comfort her. Slowly, her breathing started to steady, though she still refused to let go of me, clutching on as if I were the only thing keeping her grounded.

 THE OTHER SIDE OF HORIZON

"It's okay," I whispered again, giving her a moment to gather herself. "I'm here, Veer. You're safe. Just tell me, what happened?"

Her grip tightened momentarily, and she pulled back just enough to look at me. Her eyes were wide, glazed with lingering fear. She tried to speak, but the words seemed stuck in her throat. I gave her a reassuring nod, waiting patiently, willing her to find the words.

There was still nothing but then Veerta finally broke the silence.

"A nightmare," she said, almost incredulously, still holding onto me tightly. "It looked so real that I am not even sure if it was a nightmare."

"It was just a dream. Anyway, what could have scared my brave sister?" I asked, trying to lighten the mood with a half-hearted jest.

She ignored my attempt at sarcasm, her voice still carrying traces of unease.

"I dreamed I was in this very room when I saw a woman with flowing hair staring at me from the window." She gestured toward the window without looking at it, as if even glancing in that direction would summon the presence she described. "She reached out with her arms, gesturing for me to open the window, and that's when I snapped awake and screamed. It felt so real, Avi, and I still can't believe it was just a dream."

A chill spread through my body, digging into the core of my spine. Goosebumps crept along my arms as my gaze instinctively shifted toward the window she had pointed to. Veerta sensed that something was wrong and slowly lifted her head from my shoulder, locking eyes with me. There was a flicker of concern in her stare as she whispered, "What is it, Avi?"

I hesitated, the words teetering on the edge of my lips. Still, I asked in a voice tinged with disbelief, "Did she seem out of breath? As if she was struggling to breathe… half-frozen?"

Veerta's eyes widened, her face a mask of shock. "Yes, but… how did you know?" she stammered, her voice faltering.

I knew I shouldn't have said it. I had tried to stay composed, but the unsettling truth had slipped out. Now there was no going back. I took a deep breath, steadying my voice in an effort to keep us both calm.

"She looked at me too," I admitted softly. "You'll find this strange, but I had the same dream, Veer. The only difference was… in mine, the woman was standing outside my room's window."

Veerta's expression froze in disbelief, her mind struggling to process what I had just told her. She looked utterly stunned, as if words had failed her. I placed a hand gently on her head, trying to reassure her.

"I'm here with you," I said, my voice low and steady. "You have nothing to worry about. Now, grab your quilt. You're sleeping in my room tonight."

I helped her settle into my bed while I took a seat on the couch, opening her laptop and pretending to browse through the photos she had taken earlier. In truth, my mind was racing, trying to make sense of the unsettling coincidence that we had experienced the same nightmare.

I glanced at the time on the laptop screen. It read 12:20 a.m.

"I'm not sleepy at all," Veerta said quietly from the bed, staring at the ceiling as if it held the answers she sought. She seemed calmer, but the tension lingered between us like an invisible thread.

We began discussing the details of the nightmare, retracing every moment in search of meaning. There was one thing that troubled me from the very beginning—the woman's appearance.

It didn't take long for us to arrive at the same chilling conclusion. The woman we saw in our dreams resembled the woman from the portrait in the abandoned house. I was sure of it because I had studied that picture closely. When I mentioned it, Veerta nodded in agreement, her voice barely above a whisper as she confirmed that the figure in our dream bore an uncanny resemblance to the woman in the photograph.

Her words made my chest tighten with unease. She reminded me of the escort's warning and the ominous advice not to venture into abandoned houses.

At first, I scoffed, brushing off the nightmare as mere coincidence. But deep down, a seed of doubt had already been planted. It gnawed at the edges of my mind, refusing to be dismissed so easily.

She settled back down to sleep as the words from the escort echoed in my head. I had just experienced something incredible, and although part of me refused to believe it and dismissed it as a coincidence, a deeper part of me was unsettled. This inner conflict gnawed at me, leaving me frustrated. I glanced at the clock on the laptop and it read twenty past one. I tried to relax and closed my eyes, hoping to drift back into sleep, but it was no use. A strange tension filled the room, lingering like a fog that refused to lift.

Just as I began to succumb to drowsiness, I noticed Veerta stirring. She sat up suddenly, and the tension in her body made it clear she had heard it too—a faint creaking noise coming from outside the cottage. It was almost inaudible at first, just a slight snapping sound, as if wood was being bent or broken. But then it grew louder, more frequent, as if something was pacing around the cottage.

I sat up and rubbed my eyes, trying to shake off the remnants of my interrupted sleep. The sound became more distinct, almost rhythmic, like footsteps snapping twigs underfoot. Veerta's head darted from one direction to the other, trying to pinpoint the source of the noise. I remained still, listening carefully.

"You know how wood expands and contracts," I whispered, attempting to sound logical. "The sun heats it during the day, and now with the cold, it's shrinking again. That's all this is."

Veerta gave me a look that told me she wasn't convinced. "There was no sun today, Avi. It was cloudy all day yesterday too. Stop trying to explain everything with science."

I wanted to argue further, but before I could respond, we both froze. A new noise cut through the stillness—knocking. It was soft at first, a gentle tap against the front door. Then, almost immediately, it echoed from the back door. A moment later, the knock sounded from the kitchen entrance. The knocks moved between the doors, as if something or someone was testing them, searching for a way in.

We sat in stunned silence, tracking the knocks as they traveled around the cottage. I could feel Veerta's breath quicken beside me, her fear palpable.

"It's her," Veerta whispered, her voice barely audible. "The woman from the dream."

"It's just the wind," I said, though my voice wavered slightly. "The wind must be playing tricks, making things knock around outside."

But even as I spoke the words, I knew how feeble they sounded. Veerta's expression grew more terrified, her wide eyes glistening with tears.

"Brother, please don't go out there," she pleaded. Her voice cracked with fear as she clung to my arm. "I don't want to be alone. I'm scared."

I had never seen Veerta like this before. She had always been the strong one, braver than me in many ways. Now, seeing her like this, trembling and afraid, filled me with a deep sense of responsibility. I realized I could not leave her alone, not like this.

I took a deep breath, gathering my composure, and said, "I'm not going anywhere. I'm here, and I'm not leaving you." I pulled her close, trying to calm her down, and we sat together on the couch. She buried her face in my shoulder, her body still shaking with fear.

The knocks continued intermittently, faint taps at each door, but they gradually began to fade, as if whatever or whoever was out there was moving further away into the night. The eerie sounds grew distant, blending with the rustling of the wind in the trees until they were barely discernible.

"It's stopped," she said with a smile on her face, but she still refused to let go of me.

"I told you, didn't I? It was just the wind," I said with as much confidence as I could muster. Her eyes were hazy with sleep, but she resisted its pull. It took her

   THE OTHER SIDE OF HORIZON

another twenty minutes before she finally drifted off on my shoulder.

Gently, I shifted her, laying her down on the couch cautiously to avoid waking her. My back ached slightly as I straightened, and a thirst began to gnaw at me. I remembered the water bottle beside my bed was empty, so I made my way to the living room to fetch water.

The cottage was eerily silent as I walked through it, but just as I reached the room, I heard it again: a soft, deliberate knock on the door. It was so close, so gentle, that the sound alone might not have startled me. But then I saw the doorknob moving ever so slightly, as though someone on the other side had just tried to turn it.

In that moment, I knew. This was not the wind. I felt a shiver run through me, my body trembling slightly from the realization. The idea of turning away, of ignoring it and returning to my sister on the couch, tugged at me. But my mind wouldn't let me. Something inside demanded answers, whispered that I wouldn't be able to live with the doubt if I walked away now.

I thought of the rifle the escort had mentioned. Moving stealthily, I slipped back to my room and quietly opened the wardrobe doors. There, tucked behind some old clothes, rested the rifle. It was an old double-barrel but appeared to be in excellent condition. I carefully opened the drawer beneath it, finding a box of shells inside.

I took out six shells, loading two into the rifle. With slow, deliberate steps, I made my way back to the door. The gentle knock came again, a pleading sound, as though someone just beyond the wood was asking for entry.

Gun in hand, I pressed my eye to the peephole. The porch lay empty. There was nothing out there but the faint reddish hue of the night sky, as though the darkness had taken on a strange tint. I kept my eye glued to the peephole, waiting, listening. Moments passed in heavy silence until the knocking came again—but this time from the kitchen door.

I hurried to the nearest window, hoping to catch a glimpse of whatever was out there. But all I saw was pitch-black night. The sky was still choked with dark clouds, leaving the forest below hidden in deep shadow.

Another knock—this time from the back door.

Laughter bubbled out of me, sudden and unbidden. The absurdity of the situation had gotten the better of me, and I couldn't help but find it all strangely amusing. What was happening here? The knocking followed a pattern now, moving from the front door to the kitchen, then the back, and starting all over again, like some eerie game.

I took a deep breath, steadying myself. I needed to stay calm, keep control. The knock came again from the front door, just as I had expected. My heart raced, but my mind had made itself up. I couldn't stand the suspense any longer.

This was it. I had to confront whatever was out there.

I knew the next knock would come from the kitchen door. With my heart racing, I positioned myself at the main door, one hand on the door handle and the other gripping the rifle. My plan was to wait for the next knock, and swing open the main door, hoping to catch sight of whatever was behind the noises. The kitchen door was perfectly visible from where I stood. I only needed a split second to confirm my suspicions.

And then it happened. The knock echoed once again from the kitchen door.

I knew the pattern, and so I knew the thing was coming to my door and so with no hesitation, I yanked open the main door and rushed outside into the night, the rifle held steady in front of me. The darkness was suffocating, an oppressive void that swallowed everything. I could hardly see beyond a few steps. My pulse thundered in my ears, and for a moment, I questioned whether I was making the biggest mistake of my life.

The bulb on the porch was my only lifeline to clarity. Without lowering the gun, I reached for the switch and flicked it on. The porch flooded with light, casting long shadows that danced eerily across the old walls of the cottage.

And then I saw her.

Standing no more than three feet away was the woman from the photograph in the abandoned house. She wore the same red dress, her eyes wide and fixed on mine. Her face was pale and flawless, and her beauty, which had once seemed enchanting, now felt cold and unnatural.

Her body was caught mid-movement, as if she had been rushing toward me and froze the moment I flicked on the light. I could see the wind teasing her dark hair, but she didn't move. Judging from her posture it was clear that she was running towards me from the kitchen door and had come to a sudden halt when I switched the light on. We stood there, face to face, locked in a terrifying, silent encounter.

Then, without a sound, she began to retreat.

She moved backward, each step as smooth as if she were gliding on air. Her movements defied logic, as though her body was being pulled by invisible strings, undoing the very steps she had taken toward me. She never turned around and her face stayed locked on mine, her dark eyes drilling into my soul. One moment, she was almost within reach, and the next, she melted into the shadows, vanishing as if she had never been there.

I stood rooted to the spot, paralyzed with fear. My hands trembled, the rifle heavy and useless in my grip. I wanted to believe it was a nightmare, but I knew it wasn't. This was real, frighteningly real.

Footsteps from inside the cottage jarred me from my stupor. I instinctively raised the gun, but a familiar voice called my name.

"Avi?"

It was Veerta. She stepped out onto the porch, her eyes filled with concern. Her touch on my shoulder was like a lifeline, snapping me back into reality.

"Why are you out here? What are you doing with that gun? The sound stopped, and I told you not to go. You never listen to me," she said, her voice half scolding, half worried.

I wanted to tell her everything I had seen, but I couldn't find the words. Instead, I grabbed her hand and pulled her back inside the cottage. My entire body felt numb, and my mind swirled with disbelief. Everything I thought I knew about the world had been shattered in that single moment.

We left the cottage the next morning. I never told Veerta about what I had witnessed on the porch that night. I didn't have the courage to confront it, not then, and not now. Ten years have passed since that night, yet the memory remains as vivid as if it happened yesterday. That haunting image of the woman in the red dress still visits me in my dreams, a relentless reminder that some truths lie beyond reason.

The Happening on Richmond Road

My name is Arjun Sharma, and I serve as a columnist for *The New Line*, where I have spent the last few years covering the crime beat. I didn't venture into this profession for wealth or because I possessed some innate gift for investigative journalism. Instead, I entered this field out of a sheer, unrelenting passion for uncovering the truths that so often lurk in the shadows. From the beginning, I committed myself to one guiding principle: to write the truth and nothing but the truth.

I firmly believe that *"truth is truth even if no one believes it, and a lie is a lie even if everyone believes it."* My uncompromising philosophy earned me far more enemies than allies in the profession, yet I never cared much about that. Friendship was a distant second to integrity. Over the years, I've reported on many peculiar, even captivating cases, each one with its own twists and enigmas. However, it would be disingenuous to say that any of them held the same grip on my mind as the case of 'Veera, the Fearless.'

Veera wasn't just another criminal on the police radar, and his name came to symbolize defiance against power. Though he was wanted in connection with multiple murders across Haryana, Veera's story broke into national consciousness after he assassinated a corrupt Panchayat official along with three of his bodyguards. What made the story legendary was that he killed them single-handedly and slipped past law enforcement without leaving a trace.

I became captivated by Veera the moment I saw his story unravel on television. There was something about him that fascinated me because he was a man who had once been a college graduate with distinction, destined for an ordinary life, but who had instead transformed into one of the most feared figures of our time. Veera's story was a strange blend of brilliance and fury, with ambition twisted into rebellion, and it lingered in my mind long after the headlines moved on.

My second encounter with Veera's legacy, though, was unexpected. It was many years later, during my second posting to Shimla, that the echoes of his story came rushing back to me. Shimla, with its serene charm and ethereal beauty, felt like an unlikely stage for any crime to unfold, let alone one involving a figure like Veera. But fate, it seemed, had a way of surprising me.

Shimla was blessed with every natural bounty one could wish for. Nestled amidst emerald-green hills with their snow-capped peaks, the town exuded an old-world charm that felt timeless. The British-era architecture, with its colonial buildings standing tall like memories frozen in stone, made it feel distinct from any other hill station. I held a special attachment to this place, for it was here that my career as a journalist had first taken root.

Admittedly, Shimla wasn't the most action-packed location for a crime journalist. It was quiet and perhaps a little too quiet, but the refreshing cool breeze and the breathtaking scenery were welcome compensations. I arrived a few days before my official start date to reconnect with old acquaintances, people who had made my first stint in Shimla memorable. I hadn't yet been assigned a residence, so for the time being, I stayed at the Titla Hotel on Richmond Road, where I spent many afternoons enjoying the peace and solitude of my balcony.

That evening, I was savoring a cup of tea, watching as the sky darkened under the heavy weight of gray clouds. The chill in the air made the warmth of the tea feel like a small luxury, the kind one learns to appreciate in places like this. Suddenly, the wail of sirens echoed down the road, accompanied by the unmistakable strobe of red lights flashing through the mist. I leaned over the balcony railing just in time to catch sight of three Himachal Pradesh Police gypsies, closely tailed by an ambulance, speeding up Richmond Road.

I had heard sirens blaring intermittently for the past few hours, but they hadn't caught my attention until

   THE OTHER SIDE OF HORIZON

now. What I saw through the mist sparked a deep sense of unease. Having worked in Shimla before, I knew that such a convoy was anything but ordinary. The sight of the ambulance trailing the police cars amplified my concern. Ambulances following police vehicles rarely bode well.

A gnawing worry began to form in the pit of my stomach. The road the convoy had taken led toward the home of a close friend of mine, Vipul Jhingta. Vipul was a doctor by profession and had become one of my most trusted companions during my previous posting in Shimla. Even after I left, we had stayed in touch, our friendship surviving the distance and the years.

Vipul's house was where I had headed immediately upon arriving in Shimla, hoping to catch up before my work officially began. His wife had traveled to Delhi to visit her mother, so the past few days had been spent enjoying our old haunts, particularly a bar we both loved. The sudden appearance of the police convoy, however, shattered that sense of nostalgia and carefree indulgence.

Without a second thought, I sprang from my chair and rushed back into my room, a wave of unease pressing on my chest. I reached for the telephone resting on the side table and flipped open my worn leather-bound diary. My fingers flicked through the pages with urgency until I found the number of the local police station. I had visited it just a few days earlier while gathering information for an article.

The seconds between dialing the number and hearing someone pick up on the other end stretched unbearably, each ring hammering my nerves. Finally, the call connected. The voice on the other end belonged to the head constable, but something was off. His tone was strange, strained, almost as if he was unsure whether to say what needed to be said. I recognized him instantly, and I decided to use our acquaintance to my advantage. A few moments of friendly persuasion, along with subtle pressure, were enough to loosen his tongue. It was from him that I uncovered the reason behind the chaos I had just witnessed from my balcony.

What he told me sent a chill down my spine. A man had appeared at the door of my friend, Dr. Vipul Jhingta, seemingly out of nowhere. Vipul had been alone at home when the stranger arrived. The man, disheveled and bleeding, was in terrible shape and required urgent medical care. After pulling the man inside and taking a closer look, Vipul recognized him from the countless news reports that had circulated over the years that it was Veera.

Veera, the same elusive fugitive wanted for multiple murders, had somehow found his way to Vipul's doorstep. His haggard appearance suggested he had been on the run for days, if not longer. Vipul acted quickly, tranquilizing Veera with a sedative he kept for emergencies and then calling the local police station without delay.

Ankush Chauhan, the station in-charge, didn't waste a second once he heard the name. Recognizing the gravity of the situation, he gathered his team and sped toward Vipul's house with sirens blaring and lights flashing.

Hearing this, my heart raced with excitement. I barely waited for the constable to finish speaking before slamming the phone receiver back into place. My mind was ablaze with possibilities. This could be the story of a lifetime. Veera, the most feared criminal in the region, had not only been found but caught right here in Shimla. And I, by a stroke of luck, was within reach of the unfolding drama. It was almost too perfect to believe.

I snatched my jacket from the back of the chair, threw it over my shoulders, and headed for the door. As I slipped my arms into the sleeves, my hand instinctively checked my pocket for the car keys. I felt the familiar weight of the keys and pulled them out, gripping them tightly as I took the stairs two at a time. My steps were quick, each one fueled by the thrill of what lay ahead.

Once I reached the parking lot, I jumped into the driver's seat and glanced briefly into the rearview mirror. My reflection stared back at me, wide-eyed, slightly flushed, but alive with anticipation. I paused just long enough to take a deep breath, willing myself to calm down. A thousand thoughts rushed through my head. If Veera's capture became part of my coverage, it could catapult my career to a whole new level.

For a moment, I felt grateful for the bizarre coincidence that had landed me in the right place at the right time. My hands were steady as I slotted the keys into the ignition. The engine roared to life, shattering the silence of the parking lot. Without hesitation, I pressed hard on the accelerator, and the car surged forward, eating up the distance between the hotel and Vipul's house.

The drive was a blur, and before I knew it, I had arrived. The scene before me was exactly what I had imagined and maybe even more dramatic. Police had barricaded the area, their vehicles parked haphazardly with lights flashing in every direction, casting eerie red hues across the dim surroundings. A small crowd of onlookers had already gathered, their faces alight with curiosity and excitement. A few local journalists hovered near the barricades, eager for a glimpse of the unfolding spectacle.

The transition from evening to dusk had painted the scene with an almost cinematic effect. The police vehicles, their lights spinning in frantic loops, added an atmosphere of tension and thrill. I parked my car just outside the barricade and approached the officers guarding the perimeter.

"I'm a friend of Dr. Vipul Jhingta," I explained, hoping it would get me through the cordon. But the officer didn't budge. I even flashed my press card, but the response was the same: a curt shake of the head.

     THE OTHER SIDE OF HORIZON

I stood at the barricade, frustrated and restless, my mind racing as I tried to figure out how to get inside. Minutes passed, each one dragging longer than the last, until I saw a familiar figure emerge from the house. It was Ankush Chauhan, accompanied by Vipul, who appeared to be deep in conversation with a man dressed in a sleek black suit.

This was my chance.

"Vipul!" I called out, waving my hand high above my head. His eyes flickered toward the sound of my voice, and when he recognized me, a faint smile crossed his face. He raised his hand in acknowledgment, a small but reassuring gesture.

I watched as Vipul leaned in to speak with Ankush, his words too low for me to hear from where I stood. Ankush listened, but the way he shook his head suggested reluctance. The conversation continued for a few more moments before Ankush sighed heavily and gave a brief nod. With a resigned wave of his hand, he signaled to the officers at the barricade to let me through.

I felt a rush of triumph as I crossed the barrier, hardly able to believe my luck. Everything seemed to be aligning in my favor. I strode toward Vipul, shaking his hand warmly as I approached.

"Are you alright, brother?" I asked, my voice tinged with both concern and relief.

"It's been far from an ordinary day," he replied with a tired smile, the corners of his mouth barely lifting. "But I'll survive."

I turned toward Ankush, who stood silently beside Vipul. I extended my hand and offered my congratulations, expecting at least a brief moment of shared satisfaction. "Well done, Ankush. This is a big win. One of the most dangerous criminals, caught at last."

"Most dangerous? Not anymore," Ankush muttered, his voice heavy with regret. A deep sigh escaped his lips, the weight of it settling into the room like a lingering fog. "I wish Vipul hadn't found him."

Those words hit me like a punch to the gut, leaving me staring at Ankush with disbelief plastered across my face. There was something deeply unsettling about the way he said it. Before I could even gather my thoughts or respond, Ankush continued.

"I've already spoken with the higher-ups, and they still don't know how they're going to handle this," he added, almost as if speaking to himself.

His words made no sense. I glanced over at Vipul, hoping he could offer some clarity, but his expression mirrored my own confusion. Something was off, terribly off. Ankush didn't look remotely pleased about catching Veera, a criminal whose arrest would have been the crowning achievement for any police officer. Instead, his demeanor was grim, weighed down by an inexplicable burden. And as if that weren't strange enough, he had made no effort to transport Veera to the police station. They were waiting, it seemed, for instructions from higher authorities, a delay that only deepened my unease.

"This makes no sense," I murmured, my brow furrowing in frustration. "Why wouldn't you—"

Vipul placed a reassuring hand on my shoulder, interrupting my stream of questions. His touch was gentle but carried an unspoken urgency. "Come with me," he said softly. "See him for yourself."

Without another word, Vipul opened the door and gestured for me to follow him inside. I hesitated for a moment, a knot forming in the pit of my stomach, but curiosity and a gnawing sense of dread pushed me forward.

The moment I stepped into the living room, I was met with a scene that was chaotic yet oddly muted. A group of medical professionals stood in a tight circle, their hushed conversation punctuated by brief exchanges and nods toward something or someone on the other side of the room. The ID cards dangling from their necks revealed their affiliation with a local hospital. Scattered around the room were officers in uniform, others dressed in plain clothes, sitting uneasily on couches, their faces a mixture of fatigue and tension.

I followed Vipul across the room, weaving between officers and medical staff, until we reached the guestroom. I had been in this room before, but the atmosphere was now heavy, oppressive, as if the very air was weighed down by something unspeakable. Inside, a group of doctors in white coats encircled a bed, their gazes fixed on the figure lying there.

"Excuse me," Vipul said, addressing the doctors. "How is he?"

The doctors turned toward him, their faces grim, before shifting back toward the bed. I stepped forward cautiously, my breath catching in my throat as I prepared myself to see the infamous Veera, the man who had defied all odds, a living legend of fear and violence. But what I saw instead rooted me to the spot, sending a series of icy chills down my spine.

The figure on the bed was barely recognizable as a human being, let alone the towering, invincible figure I had imagined. What lay before me was a frail, half-dead man with skin as pale as death. His eyes, half-open, revealed nothing but the whites—lifeless and haunting. Bandages wrapped tightly around his head and arms, while tubes and pipes ran across his body, helping him cling to life. An oxygen mask covered his nose and mouth, but even with it, each breath was a labored struggle.

Gone was the image of the young, fearsome warrior who had single-handedly dispatched four men in broad daylight. What remained was a shattered husk, a body that seemed barely capable of containing life. And yet, against all odds, this man, this ghost was still holding on, defying death with every painful breath.

"Here is your Veera, the fearless," Ankush said, his voice thick with irony. The sarcasm stung, but his tone carried a deeper sadness, one that made the words sound almost like an epitaph.

I tore my gaze from the man on the bed and looked at Ankush, searching his face for answers. The expression I found there was one of grim resignation. There was no satisfaction, no pride in his capture. Instead, Ankush looked as if the weight of the entire situation was crushing him from the inside.

The image of Veera's photograph, the one that had dominated news channels just days ago, flashed through my mind. I remembered the young man in that picture, no older than his late twenties, with a height that towered at six foot five. Broad-shouldered, barrel-chested, with jet-black hair and a fierce intensity in his eyes. That man radiated strength, a figure that seemed indomitable, capable of taking on the world.

And now, in front of me, lay a man who looked as if he had aged twenty years in a matter of days. His body was frail, barely a shadow of what it once must have been. The transformation was too drastic, too surreal to comprehend. How could this broken figure be the same person who had sent waves of terror across the region?

Before I could voice the storm of questions swirling in my mind, Vipul spoke up, his voice laced with the same disbelief I felt.

"I know what you're thinking," he said quietly, his eyes fixed on the man on the bed. "But this is Veera. I was just as shocked by the... transformation. It's hard to believe that only a few days could reduce him to this."

Vipul ran a hand through his hair, the weight of the past few hours evident in his every movement. "I didn't transfer him to a hospital because I knew he wouldn't survive the journey. His body is too far gone and if we tried to move him, he'd die before we even reached the gates."

His words hung heavily in the room, adding to the suffocating atmosphere.

"He has suffered severe head trauma and spinal injuries," Vipul continued, his voice filled with grim expertise. "He's lost a dangerous amount of blood, and there are signs of heavy internal bleeding. His organs are already failing—if he makes it through the night, it'll be a miracle."

Vipul paused for a moment, as if struggling to find the right words. "And his back..." he began, his voice faltering. "There are whip marks, deep and brutal. Someone beat him mercilessly, as if..."

Before Vipul could finish, Ankush cut in abruptly. His expression darkened, and a shadow of something unspoken passed over his face.

"Leave that part out, Vipul. I've got too much on my hands already," Ankush muttered, frustration creeping into his tone. "The higher-ups are breathing down my neck, asking stupid questions. Veera's a local hero in Haryana, and he has a big following among the common people there. If they find out about his condition, they'll undoubtedly blame usfor it."

He sighed deeply, rubbing his temples as if trying to stave off a headache. "Please, just shelve that story for now. His story makes no sense anyway. I think he lost his mind somewhere along the way and head injuries can do that. Hallucinations, memory loss... You know how it goes. Honestly, it's possible the poor bastard just tripped and took a nasty fall in the dark of night. That fall is what put him in this state, not some wild story."

There was an unsettling finality in Ankush's words, as though he was convincing himself more than anyone else. His voice carried a mix of irritation and authority, leaving little room for argument. I stood quietly, unsure of what they were implying but wise enough to know that this wasn't the moment to ask too many questions.

For a few moments, silence enveloped the room, thick and oppressive. Then, Ankush spoke again, his tone now laced with the professionalism of a man trying to regain control of a spiraling situation.

"I've explained the situation to the higher-ups. For now, it's critical that this information doesn't reach the public. There's a mob of reporters and locals waiting outside, hungry for answers, and if word about Veera's condition gets out, it could spark chaos, especially in Haryana. We need time to craft a response, time to prepare for the fallout. The truth will come out eventually, but we need to control when and how it does."

He turned his tired eyes toward me, a flicker of regret in his gaze. "Frankly, I didn't want anyone from the press here and that includes you, Arjun. But Vipul thought otherwise."

I pretended not to hear the underlying annoyance in his words. Instead, we turned our attention back toward the frail figure lying on the bed. Veera's breathing was heavy and labored, each rise and fall of his chest an exhausting effort. The air in the room grew thick with a sense of waiting, as if we were all counting down the minutes until the inevitable happened.

With nothing else to do, we retreated to the couches in the living room, sinking into the silence. We sat there, waiting for Veera to finally let go, for the fragile thread of life tethering him to this world to snap. But somehow, he clung on.

    THE OTHER SIDE OF HORIZON

As the hours dragged by, several high-ranking officials made appearances, each one equally stunned by the sight of Veera in his pitiful condition. One by one, they left, bewildered and burdened, until the once-crowded room was reduced to just three people: Ankush, Vipul, and me. No one was allowed to enter or leave the house now. The only ones who remained with Veera were three medical staff, keeping a close eye on his deteriorating condition.

Vipul rose from the couch to check on Veera, leaving Ankush and me to sit in heavy silence. Minutes ticked by, the weight of the situation pressing down on us like a vise.

Then, suddenly, a voice shattered the stillness.

"He's awake! Come fast!"

The words came from one of the attendants inside Veera's room, and we shot up from the couches in unison, rushing toward the guestroom. My heart raced as I pushed through the doorway, eager to see what had changed.

Even though I had seen Veera only half an hour ago, the sight before me was enough to send a fresh wave of disbelief washing over me. His face, already pale, had taken on an even more ghostly hue, as though he was slipping further into the grip of death with every passing second. His eyes looked vacant, the flickering remnants of life dimming behind them. His pulse, Vipul whispered, was barely perceptible, fluttering like the wings of a trapped bird.

"He's traveling to the other side," Vipul murmured solemnly, the finality in his voice chilling.

Ankush didn't waste a second. He bolted from the room, undoubtedly to alert the authorities and make arrangements for whatever came next. Meanwhile, Vipul calmly instructed the medical attendants to leave, knowing their presence was no longer necessary.

As the room emptied, I stood silently beside Vipul, watching as Veera's shallow breaths grew slower, fainter. A subtle tremor ran across his cracked lips, and his eyelids quivered as though he were trying to open them one last time. Something about the movement was haunting as if Veera knew this was his final moment, a brief flicker before darkness would claim him.

I leaned closer, watching intently as his trembling hand moved ever so slightly. The motion was weak, almost imperceptible, but I saw the struggle, the last effort of a man trying to grasp something just out of reach.

"Vipul," I whispered, nudging him gently. "Look at his hand."

Vipul immediately stepped forward, taking Veera's hand in his own. He knelt beside the bed, his expression softening as he held on tightly, offering the only comfort he could to a man standing on the edge of life and death. I gave him a small nod, acknowledging the compassion in his gesture.

As Vipul sat beside Veera, holding his hand in a silent farewell, I noticed another change. Veera's lips began to move, ever so slightly, the faintest whisper slipping from between them. The sound was barely audible, like a breeze passing through cracked windows.

In a flash, Vipul leaned in, pressing his ear close to Veera's mouth, desperate to catch the dying man's final words.

Veera whispered something, his words so faint they seemed to dissolve into the air, caught only by Vipul's ear. Vipul leaned closer, responding in a hushed whisper of his own. A deep sigh escaped from the dying man's cracked lips, and his labored, wheezing breaths came to a final halt.

This was it, the end of one of the most feared and infamous outlaws of his time. Veera's tumultuous story, marked by violence, rebellion, and escape, had ended in a quiet breath that drifted away into nothingness. Shortly after, the official report was released, detailing how the police had found Veera gravely injured and how the medical staff fought for hours to keep him alive. The release stirred a predictable buzz in the atmosphere and headlines screamed about the outlaw's final hours, reporters speculated wildly, and whispers spread like wildfire through the streets of Haryana.

But none of that mattered to me. I had no interest in the carefully crafted narrative fed to the public.

What consumed me was the truth that died with the man on that bed. Veera's last words haunted me, their significance just out of reach, lost to the world except for the one person who had heard them: Vipul. He alone knew what Veera had said, and he alone had responded.

The flurry of activity that followed Veera's death didn't last long. The medical staff packed up their equipment, police officers filed their reports, and his lifeless body was carried out to the waiting ambulance under the blinding flashes of cameras. Reporters snapped pictures as if they could capture the essence of Veera in a single shot, but soon even the sound of clicking shutters faded. Vehicles revved, headlights cutting through the misty night, and one by one, they disappeared into the darkness.

Ankush was the last to leave, weighed down by the burden of paperwork and the lingering unease of a situation spiraling beyond control. He had grudgingly tolerated my presence, but I knew he would have preferred otherwise. It was only Vipul's insistence that had allowed me to stay.

After the house fell silent, I found myself replaying the scene of Veera's death in my mind, over and over again. What could have been so important to that dying man that he couldn't leave the world without whispering it? The question gnawed at me, refusing to let go. But Vipul was a close friend, and I knew better than to press him for answers yet, at least.

Vipul emerged from the washroom a few moments after Ankush had left. He looked around the room, scanning it briefly.

"Where's Ankush?" he asked, his voice carrying a note of mild curiosity.

"He left," I replied, rubbing my tired eyes. "Said something about paperwork and formalities that needed to be finished."

Vipul gave a small nod, but his mind seemed elsewhere. I glanced at my old Titan watch and it was twenty past three in the morning. My body ached with exhaustion, and my eyelids drooped, heavy with sleep. I shifted on the couch, preparing to leave.

"Long day, Vipul. I better get going, and you should try to get some rest too," I said, stifling a yawn.

But just as I stood, Vipul raised a hand, stopping me in my tracks. "Stay for a while, Arjun," he said, his voice low but deliberate. "I think we both need a drink. And besides..."

He held up an audio cassette between his fingers, the plastic glinting under the dim light. His eyes locked onto mine, the cassette cradled like a relic of profound importance. "There's something I want you to hear."

The sight of the cassette jolted me awake, erasing any trace of fatigue from my mind. My curiosity soared to new heights as I sank back into the couch, unable to tear my eyes away from that small object in his hand.

Vipul gave me a knowing look, then disappeared into the kitchen. I heard the faint clinking of glass and the sound of a bottle being uncorked. When he returned, he carried two glasses in one hand and a bottle of scotch in the other. He set everything down on the table between us, then sat across from me, facing me squarely.

Vipul poured the amber liquid into the glasses, the scotch catching the light and glowing like liquid gold. He raised his glass in a quiet toast.

"To Veera," he said softly, his voice carrying the weight of a man who had seen too much. "He was a bull of a man."

We both took a sip, the smooth burn of the scotch spreading warmth through my chest. But there was a faraway look in Vipul's eyes, as if his mind was wandering down paths too dark to share. He stared into his glass, lost in thought, swirling the golden liquid slowly.

"Twenty-five years," he muttered, almost to himself. "I've worked in this field for twenty-five years... and I've never seen anything quite like this."

Vipul sat quietly, swirling the scotch in his glass. His eyes, though fixed on the liquid, seemed far away, as if trying to pierce through something unseen, something lodged deep within the recesses of his mind. It wasn't the glass he was trying to see through, that much was clear, but rather a lingering thought that haunted him.

I remained silent, knowing him well enough to sense that he wasn't finished speaking. And I wasn't wrong.

"It was a strange end for Veera, a truly mysterious one," Vipul began, his voice low and reflective. "Just when I thought I'd seen everything life had to offer in my forty-five years, Veera shows up and shatters that belief and leaves me with questions I may never answer. It's strange, isn't it? The more we think we understand the world, the more it slips out of our grasp. There's always something out there waiting to remind us how little we know."

He shifted his gaze from the glass to me, and for the first time in years, I saw something different in his eyes. There was a restlessness, an unspoken pursuit, as if he were chasing after an answer that lay just beyond reach. His eyes weren't merely tired; they carried the burden of something much heavier, something impossible to put into words.

I sat there in silence, listening with the same intent I always did, waiting for him to continue. His words were weighed with meaning, and I knew better than to interrupt.

After a brief pause, Vipul spoke again, this time steering the conversation in a direction I hadn't expected.

"Tell me, Arjun," he said, his eyes narrowing slightly. "What do you know about the last house on this road? I remember you were working on an article about it the last time you were posted here."

The sudden change of subject caught me off guard, but I welcomed the chance to speak. It had been a while since I had thought about that house, though it had always lingered at the back of my mind like a half-forgotten dream.

"Ah, the haunted house," I replied with a wry smile, leaning back slightly in my seat. "Yes, I did some extensive research on it during my last posting here, though I never finished the article. That house is a tangled mess of history and rumors that traced all the way back to two English brothers, the Matthews, who lived there during the colonial era."

I paused, collecting my thoughts, then continued. "The brothers were as different as night and day. The younger one was gentle, kind-hearted, and known for his love of cigars. The elder brother, though, was quite the opposite: hot-tempered, distrustful, and strangely obsessed with walking sticks. They lived in that house with their families until tragedy struck in 1970. Six people were murdered in a single night, and the two brothers, their wives, and their children."

Vipul's eyes remained locked on mine as I spoke, the intensity in his gaze unrelenting. I could feel the weight of his attention, as if he were searching for something in my words.

"The story goes," I continued, "that the younger brother, out of kindness, allowed two travelers to stay the night, despite the elder brother's protests. But sometime during the night, those travelers slit the throats of everyone in the house and robbed them. The news sent shockwaves through the region, not just because of the brutality but also because of how strange the whole incident was. To this day, the case remains unsolved."

I leaned forward slightly, my voice lowering. "After the murders, people began to claim that strange things started happening in the house with doors opening on their own, voices whispering in the night. Every family that took possession of the house after that faced misfortune. There was even a man named Mr. Josh who moved in during the 1980s, only to lose all three of his children in a tragic accident just days later. And there are countless other stories regarding curses, bad luck, and strange sightings. I was planning to write a full article on it, but before I could finish, I was transferred to Delhi."

I stopped speaking and studied Vipul's face. His expression was distant, as though my words had carried him to the deepest corners of his mind.

"But what does any of this have to do with Veera?" I asked, unable to contain my curiosity any longer. "And why do you keep calling his case a mystery? What did he whisper in your ear before he died?"

Vipul didn't answer right away. For a moment, it was as if my words hadn't even registered. He stared into the middle distance, nodding slowly, as though a puzzle piece had just fallen into place in his mind.

Then, finally, he spoke, his voice calm and measured his usual tone, but with an edge of finality that made the hairs on the back of my neck stand on end.

"You think Veera was just some unlucky soul who stumbled, fell, and ended up like that?" Vipul asked, his voice low but edged with disbelief. "No, my friend. The marks on his back tell a different story for those were left by something heavy, whipped against him again and again with brutal force. Those weren't the kind of injuries you get from a fall. They were the marks of sheer torture, Multiple fractures and he had lost a lot of blood.

"But the most remarkable thing is that Veera still walked two miles to reach my house. Can you imagine that? He didn't just stand on his feet when every inch of his body must have been screaming in pain, and he still *walked*. To do that, in that condition, it takes something more than strength. It takes something unimaginable."

Vipul leaned forward, gripping his glass tightly as he continued. "I thought it was all beyond understanding, until now. Now, after hearing your version of the haunted house, things start to fit. They didn't make sense before, but they do now."

He paused for a moment, his gaze darkening as if recalling a nightmare. "One thing is certain: Veera endured unspeakable agony for days. The bruises on his back, they were days old. And as for Ankush's theory about hallucinations? That's bullshit. When Veera showed up at my door that evening, he wasn't hallucinating. I saw it in his eyes and he knew exactly what was happening. He knew his end was near. But he wasn't scared, not one bit. They didn't call him 'Veera, the fearless' for nothing."

Vipul stopped, swirling the scotch in his glass, as though reliving the encounter in his mind.

"I didn't even recognize him at first," he admitted. "The man standing in front of me looked nothing like the images from television. But when I asked for his name, he told me without hesitation. No lies, no attempt to hide who he was. He wasn't trying to escape anymore. It was like he had already made peace with his fate. And then..." Vipul exhaled slowly, as if the memory itself weighed heavy on his chest. "He told me he needed to say something important. Something he couldn't take with him to the grave."

Vipul raised the glass to his lips, taking a long, deliberate sip before setting it down with a soft clink. Then, as if reminded by an invisible thread of thought, he pulled the cassette from his pocket, the same one he had shown me earlier.

For a brief moment, I had forgotten about the tape, caught up in the new revelations Vipul had laid bare. But now that I saw it again, a wave of urgency surged through me.

"What's so important about this cassette?" I asked, the eagerness in my voice slipping through despite my efforts to remain composed.

Vipul held the tape up between his fingers, his expression shadowed by something unreadable. "I recorded everything, Arjun. I was listening to music on my Walkman when Veera showed up at my door. I don't know what possessed me, but I hit the record button the moment he started talking. And what he said—" Vipul's voice faltered for a second before he regained his composure. "What he said was beyond anything I could have imagined. He told me everything that happened to him after arriving in Shimla. Every detail. And believe me when I tell you this: the story is unlike anything you've ever heard."

Vipul's tone was unsettling, as if the truth itself carried a weight too heavy to bear. Without another word, he stood and disappeared into the next room, leaving me alone with my thoughts and the rising anticipation in my chest.

He returned a moment later, a Walkman in one hand, moving with quiet purpose. My heart raced as I watched him insert the cassette, each click of the mechanism amplifying the tension in the room. He pressed a few buttons, fast-forwarding to a specific point on the tape. The moments stretched out, each one feeling longer than the last, as if time itself was holding its breath. I emptied the remaining scotch from my glass, trying to calm the excitement bubbling within me.

This tape could be my breakthrough; the story that would catapult my career to new heights. But I kept those thoughts buried, careful not to let them show on my face.

     THE OTHER SIDE OF HORIZON

Finally, the tape began to play. A faint crackling noise filled the room, followed by the shaky sound of a man's voice and it was Veera's voice. His words came slowly, each one dragged from the depths of exhaustion, but they were clear and deliberate.

I leaned forward, my heart pounding in my chest as the recording continued. And then, Veera's story began to unfold.

"After the incident in Haryana, I somehow managed to escape and made my way to Shimla, just as I had planned. I knew the hill station well from my college days, having visited with friends many times before. Richmond Road was familiar to me, and I remembered the old abandoned house at the end of it. It was the perfect hideout—isolated, far from prying eyes. I needed somewhere remote, just for a few days, until the heat died down. And that house seemed like the ideal place.

By the time I reached it, dusk had begun to settle over the hills. The clouds drifted low and heavy across the sky, dimming the light and adding a chill to the air. I stood at the gate, my bag slung over my shoulder. Inside were a few changes of clothes, some essentials, bottles of water, and crates of tinned food and dry fruits, enough to keep me alive for a while.

The iron gate groaned loudly as I pushed it open, its hinges stiff with rust from years of neglect. I stepped through and made my way down the path, weaving between the crumbling remains of garden fences that framed what was left of a cemented walkway. The silence was thick, broken only by the crunch of my boots against dead leaves scattered along the path.

But as I approached the door, I was startled to see movement as an old man stepped out of the house and began strolling slowly toward me.

He didn't seem surprised to see me there. In fact, his presence was the first of many unsettling things about that night. I had assumed the house was abandoned, but here he was, emerging from the shadows, as if he'd been waiting for me. He wore a shabby shirt and old pants, far too thin for the cold evening. In one hand, he held a small candle, the flickering flame casting eerie shadows across his gaunt features. He looked like a figure from another time, like one of those strange characters in vintage films.

This was not what I had expected. I had come seeking shelter in an empty house, but the appearance of the old man changed everything. Still, turning back wasn't an option. The nearest inhabited house was two miles away, and venturing closer to any populated area would have been too dangerous under the circumstances. I had no choice but to adapt my plan.

I approached him cautiously, forcing a polite smile.

Excuse me, sir," I said in the most courteous tone I could muster. "I seem to have lost my way, and I have a bad leg, so I need a place to stay for the night. Is there

     THE OTHER SIDE OF HORIZON

an empty room in your quarters that I could use for the night?"

We faced each other across the threshold, the candlelight between us casting dim, wavering shapes on the cold ground. His expression remained unreadable, his pale eyes scanning mine with a quiet intensity.

"You wish to stay in this house?" he asked, his voice low and raspy, as if it hadn't been used much lately.

"Yes, just for the night," I replied in a little surprised manner but trying to sound as nonthreatening as possible.

He tilted his head slightly, studying me for a moment longer. "Yes, by all means. If this is what you desire," he said softly, as though granting a peculiar request, and with that, he turned and shuffled back inside.

I followed him, stepping through the doorway into the dim interior. He held the candle aloft, the small flame casting long, flickering shadows on the walls. The house felt as though it belonged to another era, a relic trapped in time.

The room we entered was large, with several windows, but every window was firmly shut, and not one had curtains or blinds to soften the gloom. The air inside was stale, carrying the faint scent of old wood and dust. A worn-out table stood in the center, surrounded by mismatched chairs, and the walls were cluttered with faded portraits, their details obscured by the poor light.

The furniture was hideous, tattered and ancient, as though the house had resisted every attempt at modernization. It was a place where time had stopped, leaving behind only remnants of forgotten lives.

The old man gestured toward one of the chairs with a skeletal hand. "Please, take a seat," he said with an air of old-fashioned politeness. His words were deliberate, the kind of politeness that belonged to another age.

As I sat down, rubbing my hands together to warm them, I noticed the peculiar accent in his voice. It was faint but distinct, an accent I couldn't quite place. He seemed to notice my discomfort and gave a small nod.

"I'll fetch you some tea," he said, his voice soft but steady. "The kettle is on—I was just about to make some for myself. I'm afraid it's all I have to offer."

His words carried a strange kind of hospitality, a politeness that felt both sincere and unsettling. He turned and shuffled toward the kitchen, the candlelight swaying with each step, leaving me alone in the shadowy room.

"Tea is enough, sir. Thank you," I replied, making sure my voice carried earnest gratitude.

He nodded slightly, turned, and left the room. Moments later, he returned, balancing two teacups and a saucer in his bony hands. He poured tea into both cups with careful precision. I thanked him once again, my words polite but cautious.

We sipped the tea in silence. Despite the quiet, the flickering flame of the candle on the old stand seemed to speak on its own, casting restless shadows that advanced and retreated across the walls, as if the darkness itself was alive. The old man did not sit down while drinking his tea, and I noticed how stiffly he moved. His movements were oddly deliberate, as though pain or injury prevented him from simply turning his head. Instead, he had to shift his entire body toward the sound whenever something caught his attention.

After finishing his tea, he shuffled toward one of the windows and peered through a small hole in the glass. He stood there for a moment, gazing out toward the garden gate, the candlelight throwing a distorted shadow of his thin frame against the wall.

"Are you expecting someone?" I asked, trying to break the eerie silence.

"Oh yes," he murmured, without turning. "I am, indeed. I am waiting for my older brother."

His words sent a strange chill down my spine.

"I thought you lived alone in this house," I said carefully.

At that, he turned toward me slowly, and his expression darkened. His gaze, once distant, sharpened into one of suspicion. His eyes lingered on me for a beat too long, as if weighing my intentions. Then, without a word, he shuffled back toward the table and sat across from me.

From the pocket of his worn trousers, he pulled out a small box of cigars and offered one to me. I declined politely, shaking my head. I didn't smoke, and I certainly had no plans to start now, especially under such strange circumstances.

Unbothered by my refusal, the old man placed a cigar between his thin lips, took out an old lighter from his other pocket, and lit it. The flare of the lighter illuminated his gaunt face for a moment, casting deep shadows around his hollow eyes.

As the first puff of smoke curled into the air, I leaned forward slightly, hoping to bring an end to the strange encounter. "Sir, I'm afraid the day has worn me out. If you could show me a place to sleep, I would like to retire for the night."

The old man didn't respond right away. He sat still for a moment, the cigar balanced delicately between his fingers, before rising slowly from his seat. Without a word, he plucked a candle from a nearby shelf, lit it, and placed it carefully in front of me.

"Here," he said softly, his gaze shifting toward my left.

I followed his gaze, and he gave me directions in the same deliberate tone. "Go down this passage for a bit. At the end, you'll find a staircase on the left. Climb it, and the second door on your left is your room."

I repeated his directions aloud to confirm, and he corrected me on one small detail before nodding. With the candle in hand, I stood and made my way out of the room, feeling the weight of his gaze lingering on my back as I walked into the dim corridor.

The hallway was narrow, and the silence was heavy. Shadows flickered along the walls as I moved the candle from side to side, trying to make out the shape of the recess where I stood. Finally, I found the door, opened it, and stepped inside.

The room was large and sparsely furnished. I held the candle aloft, surveying the space with caution. On a small bedside table, I placed the candle I had carried from downstairs. As I explored the room, I found two larger candles resting on the mantle shelf. Grateful for the additional light, I lit one of the larger candles, adding it to the soft glow of the smaller one.

Satisfied with my brief inspection, I lay down on the bed, my body heavy with exhaustion. Sleep took me quickly, pulling me into a deep, dreamless slumber.

But something stirred in the night.

I awoke suddenly, shivering as the temperature in the room dropped without warning. The larger candle flickered wildly, its flame dancing violently, as though caught between invisible fingers pinching the wick. The strange, erratic movements of the flame captivated me, sending a chill through my bones.

I wasn't alone.

I couldn't see it, but I could feel something in the room with me, an oppressive presence lurking just beyond the flickering candlelight. Then, without warning, a strange flapping sound echoed through the space. I froze, my pulse racing. It wasn't the sound of curtains or blinds fluttering in the wind. There were no curtains, no blinds that could explain the noise.

Suddenly, I heard the howling of wind, though there were no open windows. The air thickened, and before I could react, something heavy and malevolent pressed down on me.

Out of the darkness, an old man appeared, a man with a shining stick clutched tightly in his hand. His face loomed above me, twisted with rage and hatred. It was the face of someone who had lost all reason, consumed by madness. His eyes burned with an intensity that chilled me to my core. This was no ordinary man. I knew it in an instant—this was something far more terrifying, something not bound by the laws of the living.

For the first time in my life, I felt true fear, unrelenting fear. And the source of that fear was not a gun or a knife, but an old man wielding a simple stick.

I tried to move, tried to fight back, but my body refused to respond. Something pinned me to the bed, forcing my face into the mattress, my back exposed to the room. No matter how hard I struggled, I couldn't free myself.

The old man's stick came down on my back with brutal force, again and again. Pain seared through me, and I gritted my teeth against the agony. The blows rained down relentlessly, each one more vicious than the last.

And then he spoke.

His voice was low, filled with venom and fury, each word slicing through the air like a blade. The sound of his voice made my skin crawl, a voice so unnatural it seemed to come from the depths of some otherworldly place.

"Why did you do it?" the old man screamed, his voice filled with rage and anguish. "My brother gave you shelter, and you... Why? Why?"

He shouted the words again and again, his voice reverberating through the darkness, each scream more desperate than the last. I tried with every ounce of strength to move, to fight back, but unseen hands with a power beyond comprehension held me down. I struggled in vain, pinned against the bed, my back exposed to the brutal blows. Then everything went black.

When I regained consciousness, I found myself lying on the cold, dusty floor. I had no memory of how I had ended up there or how long I had been unconscious. The morning sun streamed weakly through cracks in the walls, casting pale light on a room that now looked entirely different from the one I had seen the night before.

There was no furniture, no candle, no old portraits on the walls, just dust, cobwebs, and decay. The house was lifeless, as if it had stood abandoned for decades. My back throbbed with searing pain, and there was blood all over the floor. Each breath sent fresh waves of agony through me, and I knew, without a doubt that several bones had been broken by the vicious beating.

Every movement was torture, and it took everything I had to climb down the staircase. I almost fainted halfway, the pain so overwhelming that I let out involuntary screams, but I forced myself to keep going. With every agonizing step, I whispered to myself, "*I am Veera.*" I repeated it like a mantra, over and over, desperate to anchor myself to the reality of who I was.

I didn't drag my broken body through that nightmare to be saved—I did it for one reason only: to tell someone the truth about what happened in that house. I needed someone to know. Someone had to hear the story."

The recording clicked to a halt, and the room around me seemed to shift back into focus. It was as if I had been dragged back into the real world against my will, torn away from the depths of Veera's harrowing tale. Time had slipped away unnoticed, and I couldn't even recall how long the cassette had been playing. I hadn't looked at Vipul once while the tape played, too absorbed in the haunting voice that spoke from beyond the grave.

Vipul finally broke the silence. "In his last words, he told me to tell his story to everyone... and to burn that damned house."

For a moment, I sat frozen, still trapped in the lingering grip of Veera's words. The story had captivated me, dragging me into its strange, supernatural undertow. A part of me believed every word—believed in the nightmare Veera had lived through. But another part of me, the rational part, began to push back.

I shook my head slightly, trying to ground myself. "Look, Vipul," I began, choosing my words carefully. "I'm not trying to insult Veera's story, but... it's hard to believe. That house has been abandoned for years—no one has lived there. I mean, it's... it's impossible, isn't it? I think Veera must have been out of his mind by the time he reached your place."

Vipul's gaze didn't waver. There was a fire in his eyes, a conviction that refused to be dismissed. "Out of his mind?" he said slowly, leaning forward. "Think about it, Arjun. Think about the research you did for your article. Doesn't the old man with the cigar and the second one with the stick sound exactly like the Mathew brothers?"

His words struck me like a bolt of lightning. He wasn't wrong. The eerie politeness of the first man, the way he welcomed Veera without hesitation matched perfectly with what I had learned about the younger brother's gentle nature. And the second man, the one who attacked Veera with a stick, seemed disturbingly similar to the older brother, known for his temper and obsession with walking sticks.

Vipul's voice lowered, carrying an edge of certainty. "Veera described those men in ways that align perfectly with the Mathew brothers. The politeness, the cigars, the stick... And what about the marks on Veera's body? Ankush himself said those were no ordinary bruises. Finger-shaped marks on his arms and ankles, as if someone had physically pinned him down. No human could leave marks like that, not even the strongest man alive."

He paused, letting the weight of his words settle between us. "The older brother must have learned his lesson after all these years. He won't let himself be tricked again, not after what happened the first time."

I wanted to dismiss the story, but I couldn't shake the nagging feeling that Vipul was right. His logic, unsettling as it was, held together far too well. I tried to find a counterargument, a rational explanation that would make sense of everything, but my mind came up empty. The similarities, the marks, the relentless rage of the older brother and it all fit together too perfectly.

The next day, I received a call from the main office, instructing me to write an article about Veera's death since I had been with him during his final moments. I knew then that I had a choice to make. Including the supernatural elements of the story would likely get the piece rejected or turned into a laughingstock and so I decided to do a spate article on the house to let go of the guilt for not sharing the real story.

          THE OTHER SIDE OF HORIZON

That afternoon, I drove to the haunted house with a photographer from the office. I wanted photographs of the house to accompany the article, hoping they would lend some weight to the incredible story.

But that evening, when I went to meet the photographer to review the photos, something strange happened.

"It's never happened to me before," the photographer stammered, his face pale with a mixture of confusion and fear. "I—I don't know how it went wrong. Please forgive me. Let's go back tomorrow morning, first thing. I promise I'll be more careful. I won't make the same mistake again."

His hands trembled slightly as he handed me the stack of photographs. My stomach churned with unease as I flipped through them, each image more baffling than the last.

He had taken four shots of the house. The first three were so blurred that the structure was nearly impossible to make out, as though the house itself had resisted being captured as its shape twisting and warping in the lens. The outlines were smeared, the angles wrong, like an apparition struggling to maintain form.

But it was the fourth photograph that truly chilled me. Though still blurry, it was clearer than the rest, enough to offer a glimpse of the house's decaying façade. The old, dilapidated structure stood slumped and weary, consumed by time and neglect.

And then I saw them.

At first, I thought my eyes were playing tricks on me. But as I squinted, the faded figures at the house's entrance came into focus, or, at least, as close to focus as the blurred image would allow.

Two figures stood by the main door.

One of them held a cigar between his fingers, his face obscured by shadows and smoke. The other clutched a stick, his posture stiff and menacing. Even through the haze of the photograph, I could sense the intensity in his stance, a figure brimming with barely contained fury.

A cold wave swept over me as realization dawned. There were two figures, one smoking, and the other holding a stick.

Those figures in the photograph were not of this world.

The Mathew brothers or whatever remained of them were still there, waiting at the entrance of that cursed house.

Story of a Stranger

It was a perfect night near the end of May, the kind of night that Manali offers as a gift to those seeking refuge from the chaos of city life. The air was crisp and cold, but refreshing, wrapping us in its silent embrace. After dinner, we drifted out of the cozy warmth of our cottage and into the open, drawn by the allure of the night sky.

A bonfire crackled to life, offering a welcome respite from the chilled breeze that swept gently down from the mountains. We gathered around the fire, basking in its warmth. Not far from us, the river shimmered in the moonlight, its surface reflecting the silver glow like a ribbon of liquid moonlight flowing between the banks. The moon, still climbing toward its zenith, was accompanied by a thousand flawless stars scattered across the sky, their brilliance untouched by city lights.

The stillness of the night was palpable, broken only by the rhythmic murmur of the river and the occasional pop of the burning wood. Even the night creatures and the trees seemed to have surrendered to the peace of the hour.

Our group consisted of fifteen people from different parts of the country, gathered here to trek the distant mountains that loomed over the horizon. Some of us were veterans, well-versed in the dangers and thrills of trekking, while others were novices, eager to escape the humdrum of daily life. We had come together, some in small groups like mine, and others as lone adventurers, each of us drawn by the promise of the mountains.

Seven boys, eight girls, and one guide sat around the fire. The guide, who had just joined us from the dinner table, was adding fresh logs to the flames. Sparks spiraled into the air as he resumed the conversation that had begun earlier.

"I know Manali like the back of my hand," the guide boasted, his voice calm and confident. "I've been leading treks for three years now and no accidents so far. I've covered most of the toughest trails in India, places so dangerous that even a small mistake could mean your doom. But I made it through every one of them. Soon, I'll be heading to Russia in search of new challenges."

There was a certain pride in his tone, but it wasn't just empty bravado. Our group, which included several seasoned trekkers, tested his words with subtle questions, probing for inconsistencies. Yet, with each question, the guide responded confidently, demonstrating his expertise. He was proud, yes, but he had the skill to back it up. As

     THE OTHER SIDE OF HORIZON

the conversation flowed, the initial skepticism gave way to quiet admiration.

We were deep in conversation, captivated by his stories, when someone noticed a stranger standing near a tree a short distance away from us. He stood there in silence, staring into the night with an air of detachment, occasionally adjusting the music on his iPod.

My friend nudged me and cast a questioning glance toward the figure.

"He's been standing there for about ten minutes," someone whispered.

"What's he looking at?" a girl asked quietly, her voice barely above a murmur.

"The moon, apparently," the guide answered, his tone light but observant. He had noticed the stranger too.

Though the guide's words were soft, the stranger seemed to hear them. He lowered his head slightly and glanced in our direction, acknowledging us briefly before resuming his vigil. He looked lost, as though searching for something out there in the darkness, or perhaps within himself.

Our conversation gradually shifted to other topics, meandering through tales of adventure and misfortune. Eventually, we found ourselves discussing the most fearful experiences we had faced while trekking. The veterans shared stories of danger and near-misses—moments when nature had revealed its unforgiving side.

Many stories were told, each one more gripping than the last. But one story, in particular, captured the group's full attention.

A veteran trekker, his voice heavy with memory, leaned forward and began his tale.

"It happened in Ladakh," he said in a grave tone. "That's where I learned the true meaning of fear. I was caught in the middle of nowhere, stranded by an avalanche."

He paused for a moment, as if reliving the terror of that day. The firelight danced in his eyes, casting fleeting shadows across his weathered face.

"For twenty-four hours, I stood face-to-face with death, trapped in a makeshift shelter while the snow piled higher and higher around me. Every time the snow shifted, it felt like the end was near as if the mountain itself was waiting to bury me. I could feel the weight of it pressing down, cold and merciless."

He glanced around the circle, his voice lowering as if to share a personal secret. "I don't know how I survived. But just when I thought all hope was lost, an army helicopter passed overhead and saw me. They pulled me out, just in time."

A heavy silence fell over the group as we absorbed the weight of his words. The fire crackled softly, filling the void left by the end of his tale.

In the dim glow of the firelight, I glanced back toward the stranger standing by the tree. He was still there, still staring into the night. His presence unsettled me in a way I couldn't quite explain, as if he carried a secret of his own, a story yet to be told.

Sighs of relief rippled through the group at the conclusion of the veteran's story. Although everyone had listened intently to the harrowing tales, it struck me as odd that most of them seemed to gloss over the crucial survival lessons buried within the stories. They were fascinated by the danger, but not the wisdom it left behind.

I shifted my gaze away from the veterans to search for the stranger by the tree, and found that he was no longer standing there. A flicker of movement caught my attention. The stranger was approaching us now, his steps soft and deliberate, as if he belonged to the shadows. A light mist of white steam curled out from under the hood that covered his head, merging with the cold night air.

Everyone turned to watch as he reached the edge of the firelight and dropped his hood.

The stranger stood tall, six feet, with a tanned complexion and a grim, world-weary expression etched into his face. He looked like a man sculpted by harsh elements, someone who had wandered far beyond the reaches of civilization. His demeanour exuded quiet authority, as if danger was an old companion. His sharp, deep-grey eyes gleamed under the firelight, hardened by experiences most of us could only imagine. The eyes that seemed to carry the weight of untold stories, some strange and unforgettable.

To everyone's surprise, the guide who had thus far held himself with pride and confidence rose from his seat and greeted the stranger with a respectful bow.

"I have the honor of introducing," the guide said, his voice uncharacteristically humble, "without any doubt, the finest trekker I have encountered in my life. He has climbed the highest peaks that seem to scrape the heavens, their crests disappearing into the dark legions of clouds. He has crossed the most remote lands and places so untouched that even the sun's rays rarely find their way in to kiss the earth."

The group stared in astonishment. This was a striking departure from the guide's usual self-assured demeanor. To hear him, a man so hard to impress, speak with such reverence for another was astonishing. All eyes were now fixed on the stranger, but he paid the attention no mind. Instead, he spoke, his voice deep and hollow, carrying a weight that demanded silence.

"What did you say fear was?" he asked, his grey eyes locking onto the veteran who had just finished recounting the Ladakh avalanche.

Without waiting for an answer, the stranger moved gracefully, settling himself on the opposite side of the fire, right beside me. His presence was unsettling but not in an aggressive way, but in the quiet, deliberate manner of

   THE OTHER SIDE OF HORIZON

someone who had lived through things that would leave most men broken.

The veteran, now the focus of everyone's gaze, looked puzzled by the question. He cleared his throat, trying to mask his uncertainty, but the stranger pressed on, his voice unwavering.

"You are mistaken, my friend," the stranger said slowly, "For you do not know fear. Not real fear. The sensation you described, being trapped by the avalanche in Ladakh was not fear."

The veteran laughed, a note of confidence returning to his voice. "You weren't there. You have no idea what it was like. The wrath of Mother Nature would make even the bravest of men tremble."

At this, the stranger's expression shifted. He glanced around at all of us, his gaze lingering on each face for a moment, as though he were sizing us up, not our strength, but the fragility hidden within us.

When he spoke again, his tone was deliberate, every word chosen with care. "During my life, I have faced death many times. I have been abandoned by rescue teams, left for dead. I have been declared dead by friends who thought I'd never return. And yet, I never felt bitterness. This life of danger, uncertainty, and constant threats is the one I chose. Those of us who walk this path make peace with death the day we set out. We know the risks. We embrace them."

The fire crackled softly, casting flickering shadows on the stranger's sharp features as he continued. "What you felt that day in Ladakh, adrenaline, panic, tension are not fear. They are instinctual reactions to danger, the body's way of trying to survive. They rise and fall like the tides, but they are not fear. No, fear is something else entirely."

He paused, his gaze fixed on the veteran, but his words were meant for all of us. "Using the word 'fear' to describe what you experienced is like using warm holes to explain the laws of gravitation. Those of us who live on the edge face hostile attacks, snake bites, avalanches and we are not strangers to danger. But danger is not the same as fear."

The group was silent, every person caught in the web of the stranger's words. His voice, low and deliberate, seemed to stir something primal within us, something we all knew but could never quite put into words.

"Fear," he said softly, "is not simply the prospect of death or pain. It is not the physical threat that haunts the mind. Fear is an unexplainable force, a power that strips away everything you believe, leaving only emptiness. It is the suffocating weight that crushes your soul, the sensation of drowning without water. It is the knowledge that something ancient, something beyond comprehension, is watching you from the shadows."

He leaned slightly closer to the fire, his grey eyes flickering with something dark and unreadable. "Real fear, my friends, is the sensation of choking on your own breath,

     THE OTHER SIDE OF HORIZON

of watching your beliefs crumble before your eyes. It is the hollow space that grows within your heart, consuming you from the inside out. Even a distant memory of fear is enough to make your body convulse, to set your soul aflame with dread."

The fire snapped, sending a shower of sparks into the night, but no one flinched. We were all transfixed, held captive by the gravity of the stranger's words.

"Fear," he whispered, "is not of this world. It is a force that arises under abnormal conditions and it causes the mind to falter, and the heart fails to comprehend the darkness that lies before it. It is the ancient power of shadows, a force older than time, one that lurks in the corners of forgotten places, waiting to claim the souls of the unprepared."

The fire crackled again, the only sound in the heavy silence that followed. None of us dared to speak. The weight of the stranger's words hung in the air like smoke, wrapping around each of us in invisible tendrils.

And for the first time that night, I understood that fear was not just a sensation. It was an entity, a living force that dwelled within the unknown, waiting patiently for the moment it could strike.

There was something unsettling about the stranger's words, and his tone with expressions induced a ghastly silence within the group. His definition of fear had transcended the usual meaning, elevating it into something far more profound, ancient, and ominous. We were all entranced by his philosophy, captivated not just by what he said, but by the way he said it, as if he had gazed into the abyss and returned with a message.

The female trekkers seemed particularly affected. There was a magnetism to the stranger's presence, his confidence, the strength in his voice, and the way his words resonated, lingering long after they were spoken. My friend Riva, unable to suppress her emotions, leaned forward. She broke the tension with the question that many of us had been yearning to ask.

"Can you share an experience," she asked eagerly, "that could help us better understand your overwhelming definition of fear?"

The stranger turned his sharp gaze toward her. His expression remained serious, though after a brief pause, the corner of his mouth curled into the faintest smirk.

"Ah, nicely done!" he exclaimed softly, as if he had been trying to dodge this question all along.

He adjusted his hood carefully, a calm settling over him, as though he were ready to fulfill her request. Our curiosity and anticipation swelled to new heights. We knew that whatever story he was about to tell would leave an indelible mark on our minds.

I noticed him slowly remove the earplugs from his ears, coiling them neatly. As he did, the moon finally emerged from behind the clouds, casting a pale silver glow over the peaks. It was as if the entire world paused to witness the moment. I gestured toward the moon, drawing everyone's attention to its quiet brilliance.

For the first time since we had met him, the stranger smiled, a rare, fleeting smile that seemed both beautiful and sad. He sighed deeply, as though preparing himself, but remained silent for a few moments longer. His gaze drifted into the fire, lost in contemplation.

And then, without warning, he began his story.

"This happened to me in the remote village of Aru, northwest of Pahalgam," he began in a low, deliberate voice. "I had been hired by two expeditors from the United States. Though researchers by trade, they were seasoned trekkers, veterans, on a mission to study the Kolahoi Glacier."

He paused briefly, watching our faces as if to ensure we were following.

"Kolahoi, the 'Goddess of Light,' is one of the most important glaciers in the western Himalayas. Millions of people in India and Pakistan depend on the water it supplies. It's Kashmir's only perennial water source, and the glacier's health is a matter of life and death for those who rely on it."

The group listened intently, the fire crackling softly as if in rhythm with his words.

"The trek was difficult, but the expeditors had strength, courage, and the will to push through. I warned them about the dangers along the way and, as expected, they faced every obstacle without complaint. We reached the glacier and completed the research without any major setbacks. But it wasn't the ascent that haunted us... It was the journey back."

He leaned closer to the fire, his face illuminated by the flickering flames.

"On our way down, we were accompanied by two local escorts, men from the village of Aru. They knew the terrain well and helped us navigate through it. However, the weather took a turn for the worse. Heavy snowfall was forecast, and we knew we had to descend quickly. Our plan was to reach the village by nightfall, restock supplies, and leave early the next morning to avoid the storm. But instead of staying in the village, we decided to spend the night at a cottage three kilometers away, to save time and avoid climbing back down to the village."

He paused for a moment, as if recalling every detail with precision.

"The locals didn't like our decision. They believed the cottage was cursed, unlucky, and even haunted. But we were practical people. Time was against us, and superstition wouldn't stop us. The cottage was old, isolated on a mountain slope, and not particularly welcoming. Its bare walls and wild garden gave it a deserted look, as though it had been abandoned for years. On our way up to the glacier, the place gave us an eerie feeling, but we brushed it off. Saving time was more important."

The stranger's voice dropped, the weight of the memory evident in his tone.

"We walked for hours that day, through relentless cold and under a sky that seemed to darken too soon, as if night were eager to descend. The clouds churned in wild confusion above us, as though pursued by some invisible force. The wind howled through the narrow trails, sharp as a blade against our faces. We trudged in silence, speaking only to make brief plans for our return. The closer we got to the cottage, the more uneasy I felt in my mind."

He paused, glancing around the group, as if gauging our reactions.

"When we finally reached the cottage, everyone was exhausted. The cold gnawed at our bones, and the journey had drained every ounce of energy from us. We gave the local escorts their instructions to return to the village, bring the mules at first light and with that, we were alone."

He leaned back slightly, his grey eyes reflecting the glow of the fire. "The cottage stood silent on the slope, its bare walls like the ribs of a long-dead beast. Weeds choked the remnants of a garden, and the faint outlines of old paths hinted at the order that once existed there. But now, it was a place forgotten by time, a place that did not welcome visitors."

The stranger fell silent for a moment, as though allowing the weight of the scene to settle in our minds.

"Inside, the cottage felt just as abandoned. The walls were bare, save for a few dusty mantels. The air was heavy, thick with the scent of decay. We lit a fire in the small hearth, trying to chase away the cold that clung to the very walls. But no matter how bright the flames burned, the chill remained."

His voice dropped to a near-whisper, pulling us deeper into the story. "We tried to rest that night, but sleep wouldn't come easily. There was something... off. A presence, perhaps, lurking just beyond the edges of perception. The kind of sensation that challenges your senses, making you feel as though you are not alone."

He looked into the fire again, as if the flames held the key to a memory long buried. "It wasn't just the cold or the isolation. It was the feeling that something in that house was not right."

The fire crackled loudly, startling a few of us, but the stranger remained perfectly still.

"We thought we had outsmarted superstition, ignored the fears of the locals. But as the night wore on, I realized that the real danger was not the storm outside..."

He paused, and for a moment, the only sound was the soft crackling of the fire and the steady hum of the river nearby.

"...It was whatever that came with that storm."

A middle-aged, sturdy man strolled out of the cottage and slowly approached us. His presence was unsettling, not just because he lived alone in this remote cottage, but because there was something about him that felt… off. We had met him before during our ascent to the glacier, and his odd personality had left an impression on us. There was an eerie strangeness to his gaze and his eyes were too intense, as if they harbored knowledge that others weren't meant to understand.

He was of average height, with a solid, muscular build. He couldn't have been more than forty-five, and though the years had weathered his face, it was easy to tell that he had been strikingly handsome in his youth. Dressed in the traditional greys and blacks of the local attire, he gave the appearance of someone firmly rooted in this remote place, as if his soul were tied to the mountains. He was clean-shaven, but his over-intense expression made him seem older than his years.

In one hand, he carried an old lantern, the flame inside flickering wildly in the chilly night air. He didn't seem at all surprised to see us standing there. In fact, he didn't acknowledge us with the slightest hint of curiosity. His puzzled eyes briefly met mine, then darted left and right, as if scanning the shadows for some unseen presence.

"You are late. Follow me," he said in a flat, indifferent tone.

Before I could respond, he turned and strolled back toward the cottage, the lantern's light bobbing slightly with each step. His demeanor left no room for questions or conversation.

We followed him through the garden gate, walking down a shabby path overgrown with weeds. The lantern's dim glow barely illuminated the twisted remnants of what had once been neat flowerbeds. As we approached the front door, the man stood aside, raising his lantern to inspect our faces as we entered, one by one. His sharp gaze lingered for a moment on each of us, as if trying to see beyond the surface.

Inside, the living room was a large, hollow space. A bow window divided into three sections overlooked the dark forest beyond. The room was mostly empty except for a few worn-out sofas and a large wooden table set near the chimney, where a fire burned brightly. The warmth of the flames was a welcome relief from the biting cold outside, but even the fire couldn't dispel the underlying chill that clung to the air.

We collapsed onto the sofas, too tired to speak, letting the warmth lull us into a brief sense of comfort. Soon, the man reappeared, bringing plates of hot food with him. We ate in silence, the fatigue of the day weighing heavily on us. After dinner, he showed us to our rooms.

The two expeditors, Tom and Jake, were assigned a room together, while I was given the same room on the first floor that I had stayed in before. Despite the fire in the chimney and the heavy woolen blankets on my bed, the room was cold, far colder than it should have been. There was an uncomfortable sensation in the air, one I recognized from my previous stay at the cottage. It was as though the walls themselves carried the memory of something unseen, something that refused to leave.

I lay under the thick blankets, but sleep didn't come easily. When it finally did, strange dreams plagued me, twisting through my mind like a cold wind. I drifted in and out of restless sleep, only to be jolted awake by a sound that sent chills down my spine, a sound I knew well.

It was the same sound I had heard during my last stay at the cottage, a strange, harmonious chiming, drifting through the silence like an otherworldly melody. The chimes seemed to shift locations, as if they floated through the walls. At times, they sounded as if they were coming from the very front door of the cottage.

I sat up, straining to listen. The night outside was pitch black, the overcast sky blocking even the faintest glimmer of moonlight. I moved to the window and peered out. The lantern at the main gate still burned steadily, casting a weak circle of light on the path below. Beyond the lantern's reach, the forest was a sea of shadows.

As I stared into the darkness, I saw them, two shadows, one behind the other, walking along the path that connected the cottage to the main trail. I wasn't surprised; I had expected something like this.

Tom was an adventure addict, reckless, always seeking thrills, and an avid photographer. From the way he had listened to the cottage owner's stories earlier, I knew he wouldn't be able to resist exploring the surroundings at night to capture the perfect photograph. And where Tom went, Jake was sure to follow. The two of them were inseparable, like mirror images of the same adventurous spirit from different worlds. Whatever reckless idea one of them had, the other was always right behind.

I cursed under my breath. Glancing at the table beside the bed, I searched for my watch. After fumbling for a few moments, I found it. The hands glowed faintly in the dark—1:00 AM. I shook my head in disbelief. I hadn't thought they would be foolish enough to venture out this late, especially in these conditions.

Muttering curses under my breath, I hurried to pull on my outdoor gear. I needed to catch up with them before they wandered too far. The last few days had been a lot of fun, and we had become good friends, but even the most experienced trekkers could get into trouble on a night like this. With the storm threatening and the terrain unforgiving, traveling at this hour was a fool's errand.

I grabbed my flashlight and bolted for the door. But as I reached the bottom of the stairs, something made me pause. A sound—soft, rhythmic breathing came from the room where the expeditors were staying.

Frowning, I pushed open the door. My heart skipped a beat as I saw Jake lying in bed, fast asleep, lost in a dream. His soft snores filled the room.

I stood frozen for a moment, my mind struggling to make sense of what I had seen. One of the expeditors was right here, asleep in bed. Yet I had seen two figures walking down the path outside and there were two figures, unmistakably human.

The sound of the cottage owner's heavy snoring drifted from the adjacent room, adding to the surreal confusion.

I had no time to waste. I shook Jake awake, shouting at him to get up. "Tom's gone! He's out there, alone!"

Without waiting for a response, I slammed open the front door and charged into the night, the beam of my flashlight cutting through the darkness. The cold wind whipped around me, and the lantern at the gate flickered ominously as I ran toward the trail, following the same path I had seen the two shadows take.

The night outside was pitch black as I crossed the main gate, the path ahead swallowed by shadows. The muddy trail snaked down the slope, merging with the mule track after about a mile. Overhead, the moon and stars were nowhere to be seen, consumed by a thick blanket of dark clouds. The wind was relentless now, sweeping through the landscape like an invisible force, and even the faintest breeze seemed to bite through my layers of clothing, sending cold shivers deep into my bones.

The beam of my flashlight cut a narrow path through the darkness, illuminating nothing but the lonely trail ahead. I moved quickly, my boots sloshing through the mud, but there was no sign of Tom anywhere. The cold air felt heavier with each step, pressing down on me, as if the night itself conspired to slow me down.

"Tom!" I called out, my voice echoing uselessly in the silence.

I dashed forward, my heart pounding faster with every passing moment, anxiety clawing at my chest. A sickening sense of dread gnawed at me—Tom was out there, somewhere, alone in the dark, with the storm closing in fast.

Then, out of the stillness, I heard a noise, a scrambling sound, like someone clawing their way up the steep slope beside the trail. I froze, gripping my flashlight tighter, and swung the beam toward the source of the noise.

There he was. A figure was climbing toward me from the side of the trail, his movements frantic and unsteady. The beam of my flashlight revealed his face—it was Tom. Relief surged through me as I rushed toward him, but before I could say anything, he collapsed against me, his body going limp.

Even though the night air was as cold as death, Tom's body burned against mine like a furnace. His skin was feverish, and he radiated a terrifying heat that felt unnatural, as though it came from some infernal source. I pressed two fingers to his wrist, searching for a pulse, and it was faint, erratic, and hard to read.

With no time to waste, I hoisted him over my shoulder and carried him back to the cottage as quickly as I could. When I burst through the front door, the others were gathered around the fireplace, where fresh logs had been added to the flames. Jake sprang to his feet as I laid Tom down on the sofa nearest to the fire.

Everyone listened in tense silence as I narrated the strange events that had unfolded. Jake immediately fetched the first aid kit, injecting Tom with medicine to stabilize his condition. Then, he sat beside him, pressing cold bandages to Tom's forehead in a desperate attempt to bring down his fever.

I slumped onto the sofa opposite them, exhausted. The room was thick with unease, the crackling fire doing little to dispel the tension that clung to the air like a shroud. Tom lay unconscious, his breathing labored, his skin burning hot beneath Jake's hands.

Minutes passed in silence. Then, slowly, Tom's eyes fluttered open. He blinked, disoriented, staring up at the ceiling as if trying to piece together where he was. His heavy breaths filled the room, and though he was awake, it was clear that part of him was still lost.

Jake's grim expression softened with relief as he leaned closer, offering a few reassuring words.

"Everything's going to be fine, Tom. We're here with you," he said gently.

Tom didn't respond. His gaze drifted across the room, blank and unfocused, as if he were still trying to grasp the reality of where he was. It was as though his mind hadn't fully returned to his body yet, leaving him suspended somewhere between dream and waking.

Then, the owner of the cottage stepped forward, his presence heavy with an unsettling intensity. He moved toward Tom, crouching beside the sofa. Without a word, he reached out and lifted Tom's right hand, his brow furrowed with suspicion as he studied the fevered flesh beneath his fingers.

In a voice low and deliberate, the owner spoke, breaking the tense silence.

"What did you see?"

The question hung in the air like a sharp blade.

Tom didn't answer. His glazed eyes shifted slowly toward the owner, as if struggling to comprehend the meaning of the words. Then, without warning, his gaze drifted away again, retreating back into the depths of whatever had haunted him on the trail.

The owner's expression darkened. His eyes, which had seemed distant and indifferent earlier, were now sharp and searching, filled with something close to fear. He rose to his feet, casting a glance at the rest of us, and spoke again, this time with more urgency.

"What did you see? Did you see *her*?"

A chill settled over the room, colder than the winter air outside.

"Tell me everything, *if you want to live.*"

The weight of the words hit us like a punch to the chest. Everyone exchanged uneasy glances, confusion and dread spreading among us. The sudden mention of "her" was both unexpected and ominous, and the threat that followed was even more disturbing.

For a moment, no one moved. The only sound was the crackling fire and the shallow rise and fall of Tom's breathing. The tension in the room was suffocating, pressing down on us like the weight of an unseen force.

Then, out of the silence, Tom coughed a raspy, painful sound that rattled his chest. He blinked slowly, as if surfacing from deep waters, and his voice was weak but audible and he finally broke the oppressive quiet.

"It wasn't a nightmare," Tom whispered, his voice rasping and weak. "Yes, I saw her or rather, I saw it."

He coughed violently, his body trembling as he struggled to continue. Jake leaned in, helping him take a sip of water. The fire crackled softly in the oppressive silence, and every ear in the room strained to catch Tom's next words.

"I couldn't sleep," Tom began, his voice faltering. "So I went to the living room to write in my diary when I heard it again, this strange, chiming sound. It was coming from outside, first from the main door, then from the garden, and after that... from everywhere. It's the same sound I heard the last time we stayed here."

He coughed again, wiping the sweat from his brow. "I had to know what it was. I went to wake Jake, but he was out cold. So I decided to go after it myself. I grabbed my gear and went outside."

Tom's voice dropped into a haunted whisper. "I was standing in the garden when I looked toward the gate and saw her. I saw a girl walking along the trail just beyond the gate and the sound was coming from an ankle bracelet she wore. It was... hypnotic. I couldn't resist. I followed her, calling out, but she disappeared into the shadows. I searched with my flashlight, and there she was again, walking off the trail, just ahead of me."

He shuddered violently, as if the memory itself had chilled him to the bone. "I don't know why, but I kept following her, like I was under some kind of spell. She led me into the woods, west of the trail, where she sat on a pile of stones, her back turned to me."

Tom's breathing grew heavier as he continued, his words barely audible. "I approached her... I wanted to ask so many questions, but before I could say anything... she grabbed my hand."

He swallowed hard, his eyes wide with fear. "Her hand was like ice—so cold it burned. It felt wrong, unnatural. And then... then she turned toward me."

A wave of panic swept over him, his body drenched in sweat. His eyes widened with terror as he struggled to complete the sentence. His voice faltered, the words choking in his throat. Jake placed a cold cloth on his forehead, murmuring soothing words, but Tom's trembling intensified.

The cottage owner, who had been watching with burning intensity, leaned closer. His pale eyes, now lit by the flicker of firelight, gleamed with urgency.

"This is important, son. For your life depends on it," the owner said gravely. "Did you see her face?"

Tom recoiled at the question, shivering uncontrollably. His breath came in short gasps, as if the very memory of that face was squeezing the air from his lungs.

"Tell me, boy," the owner pressed, his voice low but forceful. "Did you see her face? What did it look like? *Tell me everything if you want to live.*"

The room fell deathly silent, every person paralyzed by fear and anticipation. The fire crackled softly, casting flickering shadows across Tom's pale, sweat-soaked face. Finally, with immense effort, Tom managed to speak, his voice shaking with dread.

"She... she had this wild mane of black hair, all loose and tangled... But her face..." His voice cracked, his eyes filled with horror. "Her face was flat—almost featureless. Just... smooth skin, like she wasn't supposed to have a face at all."

He shivered again, clutching at the blanket draped over him. "Then... she opened her mouth, and I saw her teeth—long, black, crooked. And... and she *howled*—a sound so unnatural, so wrong, that it made every hair on my body stand on end."

Tom's voice trailed off, and his trembling hands gripped the edge of the sofa as if clinging to the last shred of his sanity. "That's the last thing I remember... The flashlight slipped from my hand... and then... I was running. And then... I woke up here."

Before Tom could say another word, his body went limp, and he slipped back into unconsciousness.

A suffocating silence settled over the room. We were all frozen, trapped in the gravity of what we had just heard. My heart pounded in my chest as I tried to process the horror of Tom's story.

The owner of the cottage leaned back, his expression grim. "Move him closer to the fire," he instructed, his tone leaving no room for debate. "No matter how hot he feels, he needs the fire's warmth."

We obeyed without hesitation, lifting Tom's fevered body and settling him beside the crackling flames. Then we sat down on the opposite sofa, our nerves frayed and our minds overwhelmed by the grim tale.

Jake and I exchanged uneasy glances. The owner's ominous questions and his insistence on the significance of "her" face filled us with a sense of dread we couldn't shake. We knew, without a doubt, that something far darker was at play here.

The owner stood up slowly and moved to the hearth. From an old wooden box near the fire, he pulled out a saber, a long, tarnished blade that gleamed faintly in the firelight. He unsheathed it with deliberate precision, holding it as if it were both a weapon and a relic from a forgotten era.

Jake and I watched in stunned silence as the man gazed into the fire, the reflection of the flames dancing in his pale eyes. In that moment, he looked like a captain preparing for the final stand on a sinking ship—a man who had made peace with the inevitable.

He turned toward us, the tip of the saber grazing my knee lightly. The touch sent a jolt through me, as if the metal carried some lingering curse. I instinctively pulled away, repelled by its unnatural coldness.

The owner leaned on the sword, his gaze fixed on the table before him. He sat down heavily, one leg on either side of the table, gripping the saber with both hands. His expression was grim, like a man burdened by knowledge too heavy to bear.

For a moment, he sat in silence, his eyes flickering between the bow-window and the door, as if expecting something or someone to arrive.

"I don't know what that dark thing is," he said quietly, his voice filled with sorrow. "But I've already lost my wife and son to her."

He tightened his grip on the saber, his knuckles white with tension. "Tom must survive the night. He must fight. Whatever happens, *do not leave the house.* She cannot enter this place, and tempts you to come out, but the moment you step outside..."

He trailed off, his gaze drifting toward the window. His eyes narrowed, as if listening for something only he could hear.

Jake and I sat frozen, overwhelmed by the weight of his words. My throat tightened, and though I wanted to ask a thousand questions, fear held my voice captive.

The owner's hand clenched the hilt of the saber tighter. His gaze flicked back to me, burning with an intensity that made my skin crawl.

"If you want to live," he whispered, "do not open that door, no matter what you hear."

"She is here," the owner whispered, his voice a low rasp that cut through the stillness like a knife. "Darkness is upon us."

There was something in his tone, an edge of dread so profound that it sent a chill straight to my core. I stared at him, feeling the weight of fear sink deep into my chest, but before I could catch my breath, his horrified gaze shifted past me, fixing on the bow-window behind us.

All eyes followed his stare, turning toward the window. The sound came first, a soft brushing against the wall outside, as if something was gliding along the weeds and tangled growth. It was the same haunting, harmonious chime we had heard before, drifting through the night like a dark lullaby.

And then we saw it.

A figure appeared just beyond the glass, barely visible through the darkness. It moved along the outer wall, its great mane of wild, tangled hair swaying with every step. My heart hammered in my chest as I realized it was exactly as Tom had described. And then I saw its eyes, two gleaming red embers, glowing fiercely in the night, staring through the glass with an intensity that seemed to pierce the soul.

Its hands pressed against the window, long fingers dragging slowly down the surface with a dreadful creaking sound. The creature didn't walk as it seemed to *glide* from one side of the window to the other, trailing the same eerie chimes in its wake. The sight of it was inhuman, unnatural and defied reason, as though it belonged to a nightmare we could not escape.

For a moment, the night grew deathly silent. The absence of sound was more horrifying than anything that had come before. Then, without warning, it howled a sickening, macabre sound that shattered the stillness and clawed at our minds. The sound crawled beneath my skin, burrowing into my very bones, and even now, the mere memory of it sends shivers across my neck and shoulders.

We sat frozen near the fire, paralyzed with fear. For a brief, terrible moment, we had forgotten about Tom, lying unconscious beside us, fighting his own battle against death. Outside, the thing continued its dreadful gliding, howling into the night as if reveling in our helplessness.

The fire crackled, its flames casting flickering shadows on the walls. We knew instinctively that the fire was the only thing standing between us and the horror outside. So we kept it burning and feeding it with wood, stirring the embers, anything to keep the light alive.

While the creature prowled outside, we stayed close to Tom, whispering words of encouragement, urging him to fight on. His body burned with fever, but we wrapped him in blankets, keeping him warm, trying desperately to anchor him to life. The night dragged on like a living nightmare, each second stretching into an eternity. We could do nothing but sit there silent, terrified and passing fearful glances at one another, as if any word spoken aloud might summon the thing inside.

We didn't dare approach the door or window. We didn't move, except to tend to the fire. The weight of fear pressed down on us, suffocating and relentless. Words cannot describe the depth of that terror and how it sank into the marrow of our bones, paralyzing both body and mind.

Then, just as we thought we could bear no more, a slender ray of daylight pierced through the window.

The thing vanished, disappearing into the first light of dawn as if it had never existed.

The room felt lighter, though the weight of the night still clung to us like a second skin. In the hours that followed, Tom stirred, slowly regaining his strength. His fever broke, and color returned to his pale face. Relief washed over us, but it was a hollow kind of relief—one tinged with the lingering knowledge of what we had seen, of what we had endured.

And that's when I felt the true, horrifying essence of *fear*.

Not the fleeting kind of fear that comes with danger or the unknown. This was something far more sinister, something that penetrated my soul, gripping me so tightly that it altered the very fabric of my being. It was a fear so overwhelming that it drained the life from my heart, leaving me hollow and broken.

In that moment, I understood what it meant to surrender completely and to feel your mind unravel, to be ready to welcome death as a release from the unbearable weight of terror. My body, my heart, my soul were prepared for the magnitude of what I saw in that window.

That night left a scar on my mind, one that has never healed. It still follows me, creeping into my thoughts when I least expect it. No matter how much time passes, I know I will never escape it."

The stranger's voice dropped to a whisper, his haunted eyes glancing around the group. "And that, my friends," he said, "is what fear truly is."

His gaze settled on the girl who had asked for the story. She sat in stunned silence, her heart pounding so fiercely she thought it might burst from her chest. Her hands trembled as she tried to calm herself, but there was no comfort to be found.

In the stranger's eyes, she saw something she couldn't unsee; A truth that shattered every belief she had held about the world. The certainty she once had, the knowledge she thought she possessed had all crumbled before her, leaving her with the dreadful realization that everything she had known was little more than a fragile lie.

The fire crackled softly, casting flickering shadows on the walls. But the warmth it provided felt distant, unable to reach the coldness that had taken root in her soul.

And she knew, with unsettling certainty, that she would never see the world the same way again.